Planeterial

By DW Beam

Published in the USA in 2017 by
DW Beam Publishing, King, NC
Copyright © 2017 by DW Beam

ISBN: 978-1-943455-07-2

Cover Design ©2017 DW Beam

Edited by DW Beam Publishing

This book is a fictional work. Any resemblance to actual people, places, or events is unintentional.

Author's email: dwbeam@dwbeampublishing.com

Chapter 1

The Great Awakening

Thealopium Gel, a one inch glaze outside of his body. He is awakened out of a deep sleep. A woman by the name of Glyria is spraying him off with a liquid-like substance from head to toe. She removes a tube out of his throat manually that kept oxygen in his lungs and CO_2 out. As he takes in his first breath, gasping for air, she rinses the rest of the gel, what is left, out of his eyes. Then, she rinses his ears off.

"Dr. Laveman, can you hear me?"

At first, all he can do is groan.

"Dr. Laveman, wake up! Can you hear me?"

She finishes rinsing off his head. "The station is crashing!"

"What? What did you say?"

"I said the station is crashing," she repeats.

"That's impossible! The Planeterial cannot crash! It has over a million sensors dedicated for each telemetry known to man. It has safeguards on every sensor. It has fifty-five force fields that will withstand any asteroid field and will retract any comet."

As he speaks these words, humility hits his heart as he instantly thinks back. He has spent hundreds of heaps in cryogenics, but he has been awake all together around ninety-five heaps.

They were in the beta galaxy 2915. It was named after the heap it was discovered. They were in the solar system Teve 606 on a planet called Mave. Asteroids had been hitting Mave for several heaps, but this time it was different. The planet was being destroyed.

Because the asteroids were hitting on the far side of the planet, it was causing rotation to speed up, but this heap, larger asteroids hit, causing the rotation to spin even faster on Mave, increasing gravity which caused it to be impossible to do the simplest tasks. Also, causing destruction from tidal waves, hurricanes, and earthquakes. This particular storm destroyed over a million people. By the end of six leans, over six million people starved to death.

When there was catastrophic destruction, there was an emergency broadcast, and the other parts of the world would come to the rescue. Each heap, the satellites were taken out of orbit, out of the trajectory of the asteroid belt, and then placed back for the radio communications, but when the rotation sped up, it put the bombardment in a different place, destroying all the satellites.

With satellites being down, there were no space craft with GPS that would go outside of their boundaries. No one knew that the other side of the world was starving. They were dependent on the satellite communications continually. It wasn't long before the communications were re-established, but by this time, millions of people had died.

They had been expecting this for heaps, and that's why they had decided to build a space station. Dr. Laveman was a young man. They had begun to build the ship outside of the planet on the inner rotation toward the sun outside of the asteroid belt's reach. Unfortunately, the planet was in the asteroid belt's trajectory, but the ship was in a safe spot that avoided the asteroids. They had come to the conclusion that because of the lack of resources remaining on the planet they had to leave as soon as possible. In a few short heaps, it would be uninhabitable.

The space ship was almost complete, and Dr. Laveman was speaking to his team. "That ship is indestructible. It has so many safe guards. I'd stake my full reputation on it."

Being that Dr. Laveman has an immeasurable IQ and developed and engineered most of the space station including its navigation systems, warp capabilities, and its sophisticated computer technology, as he remembers his words, his somewhat prideful statement is swallowed up as he speaks them again to Glyria.

"What heap is it?" he asks.

"It's 3523."

"We've been traveling for five hundred heaps. Something is wrong! We should have been there by now."

"That's why I'm waking you up, Doctor. The station has entered into some kind of wormhole or time warp. I don't know. The log is not really clear. All I know is that systems are breaking down, and we are heading for a straight collision with an astronomical star in a solar system of twenty-three planets," she quickly explains.

"Quick! Help me get dressed!" He can hardly move his limbs. "Who else is awake?" he asks her.

"Just you and me. The captain was awake, but unfortunately, something went wrong."

"How long have you been awake?" he asks.

"Fifteen moments now. I've been trying to bring you out of a deep sleep. I have two other doctors coming out. You will have to assist me. One has already passed away. The systems are failing and shutting down. There are over a thousand people on this vessel, and if we do not do something in a hurry, we are going to lose half of them."

"Quick! Press red alert! The system will go into de-cryogenic mode where we will not have to manually wake everyone," he tells her as he begins checking all the systems.

"Won't that put us into self destruct?"

"I'm afraid it's too late for that. The vessel is done for. The navigation computer is burnt completely up. There is nothing that can be done."

Some of the cryogenic pods have malfunctioned, and the computer has taken them out of hibernation mode. One, being by the name of Sparks. The computer opens the door, and the thealopium gel is sprayed off by an electronic arm controlled by the computer while another one removes his oxygen tube. As he begins to wake up, he keeps mumbling, "What's going on?"

The computer says, "Dr. Sparks, the reason you are awake is due to a malfunction in your cryo-pod. I was unable to analyze it because there is something wrong with the systems."

"Oh no, that's not good!" Sparks exclaims. He quickly looks over at the pod beside him as terror begins to strike.

The computer says, "I'm afraid the ship is crashing. Navigation is down along with vital resources for the survival of the ship's crew and passengers."

"Quickly! De-cryogenilize my wife! Hurry, do not waste any time!"

"Yes, Dr. Sparks, I will do that immediately."

As the robotic arms begin to take his wife out of hibernation, Dr. Sparks gets a little more excited. He starts spraying off the thealopium gel from her body because the arm is moving too slow. As the tube is removed from her throat, he begins to call out her name. "Julia, Julia, wake up! Snap out of it! We are in deep trouble here!"

4

Now, Dr. Sparks and Julia are part of three teams on the ship. One is the medical team. Another one is cultivation, which they love the most, and they are also assigned to help those on the navigation crew.

Sparks begins to shake Julia as her eyes roll back in her head and she passes out. "Oh no, what is going on?!?" he asks the computer.

"It seems she has gone into some type of seizure," the computer says over the loud intercom. "Quickly, get her to the emergency pod. She is not breathing."

Dr. Sparks grabs his wife as quick as he can. He is weakened from the cryogenics. He says, "I can't lift her!"

That's when a robotic arm pushes out a small cart that levitates and lowers down to the ground. He rolls her onto the cart as fast as he can. After energizing the levitation of the cart, he quickly presses on, still weakened by the hibernation.

As soon as he enters into the medical facilities, the robotic arms begin to help get Julia into the emergency pod. The computer quickly induces CPR. "Dr. Sparks, I am afraid I am going to have to induce electrical shock. Your wife's heart has stopped, also."

"Quickly! Don't ask me questions! Get her back to life! Do what you have to do!"

"Yes, we are working on it as we speak," the computer replies.

After electrical shock is induced into her chest, her heart starts beating, and she spits out a breath with some thealopium gel. Apparently, some had gotten into her lungs to keep her from breathing. After he sees his wife come back to life and that she is going to be okay, Sparks drops to the floor with not one drop of energy.

A robotic arm puts a shot into his chest, shooting him full of adrenaline, along with his wife. "Quickly, doctor, there is no time to waste. We are not able to analyze the problem with the navigation. The navigation team needs to be woken up, but there is something wrong with the communications," the computer tells him.

After Dr. Sparks and his wife are fully dressed, they make haste to the navigation room. Upon entering in, Sparks locates the damage right from the start. There is a hole in the ship. Robotical arms have sealed the hole with some kind of foam, allowing the atmosphere to come back into the compartment where the navigation computer is, but the computer is shot.

"Quickly, Computer, how many people are awake?" he asks.

"Including yourself?"

"Yes," he replies.

"I am not sure. Maybe ten or so. Computer systems are malfunctioning ship wide including the main computer."

"Computer, do you know how long we have?"

"Not exactly. We are on a collision course with a star or maybe even one of its planets. We are going to come close to the third planet. It seems we have maybe a spot. At the most, two spots."

A spot is about twenty-three hours, a little less than an Earth day. A rest is seven spots. A lean is about forty days. There are ten leans in a heap. A heap is a little more than an Earth year. A lean is a little more than an Earth month. How this came about no one remembers, except for the computer, and no one has had the need to ask for this information.

"Why is the computer malfunctioning and shutting down?" Sparks asks.

"Due to the surface of the solar system's sun being far hotter than any sun although it is the smallest on record," the computer answers.

That's when Sparks realizes the computer is not speaking right or acting right. He says, "Quickly, Computer, run self-diagnostics. Analyze and locate the damage to the main core processor. Figure out what's going on."

After a few seconds, the computer comes back. "Self diagnostics indicate: main computer destroyed, secondary computer, thirty percent damage. Three hundred onboard computers are relaying precise detailed data. The thirty percent damaged secondary computer is sending illogical data."

"That explains your personality gap," Sparks says.

"It is being repaired, Doctor, as we speak. Unfortunately, all of the repairs cannot be completed because the secondary main computer is continually downloading data to the on board computers. It needs manual repair."

"Great, our computer is confusing our computers. First things first," Sparks says.

He looks at his wife next to him. "Julia, are you okay?"

"I'm not sure. I am really just now getting my wits about me," she answers. "I'm not sure what's going on."

"The ship is crashing. If we don't do something in a hurry, we may perish. Quickly, let's get to life support! There is nothing we can do here. The centrifugal backup of navigation is completely destroyed including the main computer of the navigation room."

They go two flights up and enter into a great big room where there are other computers over the life support. Sensors are going off everywhere. One by one, lights light up on the circuit board. They are all mostly green. Some are blinking orange, and some are blinking red.

"Sparks, what does this mean?" Julia asks.

"It means they are about to die, these sensors that are blinking red. If we don't do something in a hurry, they will die. The ones blinking orange are about to turn to a blinking red. Once they do and the red stops blinking and turns full red, they will die. For now, there is only a handful. Quickly! Read me off the panel number of those that are blinking red so I can go locate that pod! We will do those first. I will have to manually take them out of cryogenics."

The first pod he comes to is Tarvin Dasin. As soon as he gets there, he slides his finger across the panel and mashes the red button. Decryogenics is started. As the main robot begins to start the de-cryogenic process, he yells out, "Quickly, give me the next number!"

As fast as Sparks can, he goes to each pod and takes them out of cryogenics, one after another. After he gets to the last pod that is blinking red, he starts on the orange. There are slightly more orange than he can handle by himself. When he gets back up to the front where Tarvin Dasin is, he says, "Quick, Mr. Dasin, help me with these pods as quick as you can!"

When Mr. Dasin hears this, his motivation is a little stronger although he is still weakened and in shock from cryogenics. Confused or not, all he can think about is his sister. "Doctor," he yells, "the pod next to mine, it's my sister. Please!"

That's when Sparks stops on the pod that he is on and runs over as fast as he can. "Julia, pod number 1162?"

"It's a green light. It's good," she tells them.

He yells out to Tarvin and says, "She's okay. She will be fine. You can take it out manually. Others are dying." He runs back to the pod he was on before and finishes manually taking it out of cryogenic mode.

After a short while, Tarvin is able to move, and he wings his way over to his sister's pod. He looks at it, confused at first, and he yells out, "What do I do?!?" After seeing several computer buttons, he becomes extremely excited and yells out again, "Doctor, what do I do?!?"

8

Sparks is now a good ways away. After Dr. Sparks' wife yells his name several times for each pod, Tarvin screams out one last time as he runs, "Sparks, Dr. Sparks!" That's when he gets his attention. "What do I do?!?" Tarvin repeats his cry. By this time, he has already ran halfway to where Sparks is.

"Come here, quickly! Let me show you how to do this. You are going to have to help!" Sparks tells him as he takes his finger and slides it across the computer screen at the top. "You slide your finger like this. When the red light lights up at the end, you mash the red button. Once the red button is mashed, the robotic computer will take over." After he mashes the red button, nothing happens. That's when Sparks jerks the panel down and manually releases the pod.

After Tarvin looks down at all the pods, he kind of goes into shock. "We have to do all these?"

Sparks grabs him by the shoulders. "Pull yourself together! I need you to be calm, cool, and collected and help save them. As Julia, my wife, yells out the pod number, I need you to go to that pod. She will yell one, and you will go to that one. When she yells another, I'll go to that one. I'll do one while you do the other."

"Okay, but first I need to get my sister."

"Quick, we don't have much time!"

Julia yells out, "Some are going into the red, Sparks! We are going to have to hurry!"

"Quick, yell out the number!" he tells her.

As Tarvin runs back to his sister, he hears Julia yell her pod number. That's when he goes frantic and thinks to himself, "Oh no! That's my sister's pod!"

Without hesitating, he gets back to her pod as quick as possible. He takes his finger and slides it across the top of the computer screen that is five by five inches. After he slides it, the red light does not come on. He yells out, "Sparks, the button did not appear! Dr. Sparks, the light did not come on!"

By this time, Sparks is too far away to hear. The corridor goes around as it goes farther away. Julia is over the intercom, but she is close enough to hear Tarvin. He is going into hysterics. "My sister is dying! Someone help! I can't get this to work!"

That's when Julia stops what she is doing and runs over to the pod where his sister is. "This is one of the pods you yelled out. I can't get it to work!" he frantically tells her.

She slides her finger across the panel as she is supposed to, waiting for the red button to appear to mash. It never does.

Now, being an aviation engineer and a pilot, Tarvin gets his wits about him. That's when he remembers Sparks jerking the panel down. He jerks the panel open and finds a manual release to the lid. As soon as it pops, he grabs the lid and begins to manually open it up. As soon as the lid reaches four inches up, computer arms begin the de-cryogenic stage.

Julia tells him, "Back up. The computer will do the rest."

After a moment or two, the computer arms have his sister sitting up on the side of the pod. "Why, she's just a little girl!" Julia exclaims.

"This is my sister," Tarvin says.

That's when Sparks yells out, "What's the next pod number? Quickly!"

After Julia reaches the panel, four of the blinking red lights become a solid red. She calls out those numbers as quick as she can. By this time, Sparks is exhausted. He has not been out of cryogenics long, and the adrenaline is wearing off.

Now the shock of the cryogenics takes about a sector, about four Earth hours, to wear off without adrenaline. Tarvin does not have adrenaline, but the fear of losing his sister gives him more than adrenaline. After seeing his sister is okay, he says, "I'll be back, Little Bit. I have to help this doctor. I will be right down the hall here."

As fast as he can, he jogs down to where Sparks is. Julia yells out the next number. He gets to the last one just in time to watch him perish. That's when Julia goes into shock. They all turn red. She stands back from the panel, takes in a deep breath with her eyes wide open, and yells out, "Sparks, they're all red!"

That's when Sparks realizes, "I can't save all of them!"

As soon as this happens, red lights go off all over the place. It is a red alert. All the lights turn green on the panel. The computer kicks in and says, "De-cryogenics is now in operation. De-cryogenics is now in operation."

After hearing the computer say this several times, Sparks sits down where he is at, exhausted. "Are you okay, Doctor?" Tarvin asks.

As he takes in a deep breath and lets it out, he shakes his head and says, "Yes, let's check and see how many fatalities there are."

There are two pods close by. One is a young beautiful woman. The tube is removed from her throat. But she is not breathing, and her heart beat is not there. Dr. Sparks says, "Quickly, find somebody else, and bring them to the medical bay! Maybe we can revive some of them." As he rushes past Julia with the young woman in his arms, he tells her, "Quickly, get the emergency pod ready!"

She runs on ahead, and by the time he reaches the medical facilities, she has everything prepared. He throws the woman right in there and gives the command, "Quickly, Computer, resuscitation, quickly!" The computer begins CPR and electrical shock treatment. At first, nothing. Sparks says, "Do it again!" A second shock is introduced. The heart beats twice. That's when

Sparks says, "One more time!"

After the third time, the heart starts beating but very faintly. "We have a weak pulse," the computer says. "Very weak. She is not breathing. There is something in her lungs."

The computer sends a tube-like robotic arm down her throat. There it finds the thealopium gel that had seeped down into her lung. After the robotic arms vacuum it out very carefully, her heart stops again. This time, she turns blue. CPR is introduced once again along with electrical shock. This time, her heartbeat starts as it should. She is getting oxygen.

After a few moments, the computer analyzes her breathing, takes off the mask, and stops breathing for her. That's when she begins to choke. Thealopium gel is still coming out of her nose as she begins to cry.

The pod opens up, and Julia, Sparks' wife, asks her, "Are you okay?"

That's when the main computer comes over the intercom. "Secondary main computer down to thirty percent. Imminent shut down in twenty moments."

Every pod, every machine, every facility has its own computer. Every section on board has a main computer, a secondary computer, and then a computer for each essential function, such as life support, space suits, etc., but overall radio communication, navigation, and overall life support are pretty much operated from the super computer in the main computer room which is over the whole space station. This computer was destroyed due to malfunction. Now, with its secondary computer down to thirty percent, Sparks realizes he will have to do manual repairs, and he realizes he is going to need help as he thinks to himself, "After I finish here."

Sparks leaves Julia with the young woman. As he passes

through the corridor, here comes Tarvin with a middle aged man, struggling to get him to the medical bay. His wife is helping the best she can. Sparks grabs a hold of Dr. Hollis' other arm while his wife faints to the floor. They get him into the medical bay and begin resuscitation.

Sparks yells back out into the corridor, "Ma'am, are you okay?"

"Yes, I don't know what's going on. I feel weakened," she answers.

That's just the cryogenics. It will wear off," he yells as he runs by her.

People are waking up from cryogenics by this time all over the place, in hysterics. As they wake up with the red alert going off, it hits their hearts. Those that have already been awake for a while have already heard the news and are trying to calm the others down. It is chaos!

People are asking their computers questions, but the link up with the main computer is having problems, relaying different messages than what others are telling. There is mass confusion. They have no quarters to go to. Even though they do, the computer does not know where they are, being that the main computer provides that information.

After doctors, scientists, technicians of every kind, aviator engineers, and pilots are woke up, they are assigned to their posts manually by their senior officers and those in charge. The more they find out about what is wrong with the ship, the more people are dispatched to do their duties and jobs, such as the repair to the main computer. Most of these have families, so their main concern is their family first, realizing that without their families, there is no future anyway.

Chapter 2
A Place To Live

"Dr. Glyria, I do not remember you." Dr. Laveman asks.

"I was one of the last to be put into hibernation. I am sorry I did not get a chance to meet you beforehand, but it was almost a rest after you went into hibernation that the station was set on course. Everything we needed was on that navigation computer, Dr. Laveman. What about the backups?"

"There were several backups," he answers. "It looks like some kind of gamma radiation blast hit us. Opelinium nitrate is what the computer processors were made from. They will withstand nuclear radiation, but it appears that gamma radiation shot a hole about one foot in diameter that went through the computer processors, the backups, and the warp drive on the backside, also killing somebody on the next level by destroying life support on their cro-pod. That's the reason I say the station is done for. There are five hundred escape shuttles. Two to five people can fit into each one. Each ship is equipped to sustain life."

"Dr. Laveman, I'm scared. There are no planets around that can sustain lives. This solar system is a dying solar system, and the station is creeping through. I'm afraid we're going to end up being pulled into that sun."

"We have roughly got two rests. With life support being damaged, we've roughly got one rest. We will have to work fast. We are going to have to find a planet that will sustain life," Dr.

Laveman tells her. "There are twenty-three planets here. With the navigation computers out, everyone will have to fly their escape shuttles manually until they hit an atmosphere, then the navigation computers on the ships will take control. We will have to lay out the telemetry for each vessel to reach whatever planet we choose. God help us find one!"

Now, Gretam Sortman is the captain over the ship. For some reason, his pod is the last to be revived, mainly because it is in captain's quarters. There are two captains over the ship, Gretam and Tamron Lafi. Captain Lafi perished while in the navigation room when the gamma radiation blasted a breach in the hull and through the navigation equipment. Apparently, he was sucked out during the hull breach. The captain's crew is already awake, but they could not get into captain's quarters on the space station for security reasons. The captain's pod should have been the first to wake up, but it was not. So, after they could not get in due to high security, they figured that he had died.

After a while, the android robot on the captain's shuttle got partial link up with the secondary computer for a short time. Going over to the captain's cryo-pod and seeing that it was in de-cryogenics mode but nothing was happening, the android took the panel, opened it up, and manually released the captain from his pod. The robotic arms came down and revived the captain.

Everybody is running around trying to figure out what to do. They have been trained for this, but it was highly unsuspected that it would ever happen. Calm, cool, and collected, the captain gets his wits about him and steps out onto the command post.

"Computer, status," he orders.

The computer does not answer.

That's when the second in command sees the captain across the command post entering in and says, "Captain, you're alive!?!"

"It appears to be so, as far as I can tell," the captain responds.

Now on this vessel, there are two sets of captains and commanders. The commanders are like captains. They are second in charge. The captain says, "Quick, Commander, status report."

"From what we can tell, the ship is crashing into a solar system's sun," the commander explains.

"How long do we have?" the captain asks.

"Not very long, maybe a rest."

"Get people together, and get them prepared for the shuttle craft."

"Immediately, sir, but we have already started that. We thought you had perished."

"How long has everybody been awake?" the captain asks.

"A quarter of a sector, sir," the commander answers.

After the commander gives the captain a full update and the cryogenics wear off, the captain commands a meeting. The red alert is still going off after a quarter of a sector. "Commander, do something about that red alert. It is nerve wracking," the captain demands. That's when he goes over to one of the computer panels and puts in the order to terminate the red alert.

After calling a meeting, some of the top scientists get together including Dr. Laveman and Glyria, who were the first to be woke up. Glyria being the first, except for Captain Lafi. As to why, the computer cannot acknowledge. The captain begins to interrogate Glyria as to why her pod was selected to be the first to be woken up.

That's when Glyria speaks up and says, "Well, I am the scientist over re-habitation."

The captain says, "Yes, I understand that."

"Well, apparently Captain Lafi woke me up. He analyzed the

gamma blast hitting the ship and realized that it was going to perish. I guess he woke me up first to get me started trying to find a planet suitable for life. I'm not sure that is what happened, but that is what I gathered from the logs. But after the gamma blast hit navigations, along with the only other person awake, which was the captain, that is when I went to Dr. Laveman to wake him up."

"Why did you go to Dr. Laveman and not come to me?" the captain asks her.

"I had no authorization on the command deck. The computer was down, and there was no way to get to you. Dr. Laveman was head scientist over all of us. He was also head coordinator over the whole ship, designing most of the most important parts of the ship, including the computer, and he had authority to enter the captain's quarters."

"How would Captain Lafi know the ship was going to be destroyed?" another scientist asks.

"He didn't know for sure," Glyria says. "The computer said there was a one hundred percent chance that the sun's gravity was going to pull us straight into it, and the ship being the immaculate size that it is going at light speed couldn't exactly dodge the sun's solar gravity. The captain took us out of warp drive and got us slowed down just in time as we entered into this solar system. That's when hundreds of gamma blasts zoomed by the space station one by one from the inner core of the galaxy, and then everything shut down and came back on. The captain's log said he was going to the navigation station to re-engage our navigation. He was never heard from again," she says as her eyes water up.

That's when Dr. Laveman speaks up and says, "We've got a bigger problem. Even if we get to the space shuttles, we will not survive in the heat of this solar system, and none of the planets appear to be inhabitable."

The captain says, "Well, Doctor, then we are just going to have to find a way. Now aren't we? I'm leaving it up to you and Dr. Glyria to find us a safe haven. If you have to go without sleep or eating and work around the spot, I think it is necessary. There are fifteen hundred lives depending on us. Failure is not an option. That goes for the rest of us, also. We are talking about our survival. We are the last of our kind as far as I know," the captain tells them.

"Dr. Laveman, I also want you to figure out why we are a couple of hundred heaps past our destination," he continues.

Dr. Laveman says, "It may not be so. The computer is malfunctioning. I wouldn't trust the integrity of any data unless it is from one of the space shuttle's computers. The integrity of the secondary computer was affected by the gamma blast and the radiation."

That's when Glyria collapses to the floor.

Earlier, Glyria woke up with a robotic arm helping her sit up on the side of her cryo-pod. There was no one around so she knew right from the start that something was wrong, mainly because the captain was usually standing beside her pod when she was awakened.

During the captain's shift, he would wake up Glyria, mainly because they had a secret love. He would wake her up one heap out of the five that he was awake during his shift. The captain was reluctant to let anyone know about his affair with Glyria, mainly because his daughter...well... he knew she wouldn't understand. Him being married or having a relationship with another woman besides her mom just didn't seem right to her, but after many heaps of being a widower, the captain decided it was better not to tell his daughter until he reached the new planet. Relationships between the command and the crew were strictly prohibited, especially for

18

the captains.

"Computer, why am I awake?" she asked.

The computer acted funny and said, "Because you have been de-cryogenilized."

"What?!" she asked with surprise in her voice. "I know that, but why have I been de-cryogenilized?"

The computer hesitated to answer. As a matter of fact, she was beginning to wonder if the computer was going to answer at all. Then, she said with a stern voice, "Computer!"

That's when the computer came back on and told her, "The ship is caught in the gravity of the star in the Y2DB star system, and as to why you are awake, there is no data available."

Still puzzled as to why the computer did not know why she was awake, she went straight to the captain's quarters. She said, "Quick, computer, open the captain's doors."

"Dr. Glyria, you are not authorized to enter the captain's quarters."

"Override," she commanded.

"Under whose authority?" the computer replied.

"Under my authority," she demanded.

"There are only three positions on board that are authorized to go into the captain's quarters, and you are not one of them. The captains, commanders, and head of the scientific department are the only three."

Captain Lafi had given Glyria authority, but now it seemed the computer was no longer aware of this. Something was wrong, and where was the captain?

"Quickly, Computer, where is the head of the scientific department?" she asked.

"In Department 43, Level 50, but you better hurry. His pod is not operational. He is dying," the computer answered.

As soon as Glyria heard this, she ran as hard as she could, still spitting up some of the phlegm from the cryogenics as her breathing got deeper from running with pain deep in her chest. That's when she yelled, "Computer, open the the doors to the scientific department."

The computer came back and said, "You are unauthorized to enter this department."

"This is my department," she yelled. "Override!"

"Under whose authority?"

"Dr. Glyria Upstrom, Section Number Beta Three Four Alpha Eighty-six Seven B Three. Now open these doors immediately!"

As soon as she reached the pod, the fluid had already been drained, and the tube down Dr. Laveman's throat giving him oxygen was now the same tube that was killing him. She knew she had to work fast. She slid her finger across the panel and then mashed the red button. Then, she ran to the next pod. It was too late.

Across from there, she saw that there was a red light blinking. "Stabilization, Three percent," the pod announced. As quick as she could, she slid her finger across the panel and mashed the red button. After this, she ran back over to Dr. Laveman.

In the meeting as Glyria collapses, the captain yells, "Quick, take her to the medical facilities!" Dr. Laveman assists. After entering into the medical facilities, they place her into the emergency pod and begin analyzation. She has severe radiation poisoning.

Earlier, during Glyria's search for the captain, the hall to the navigation room was filled with radioactive material. The reactor, because of the sudden halt, put out an extravagant amount of radiation through the hole that had gone through the navigation room, flooding the hallway with the radioactive material. Glyria, not knowing this, had passed right through it. After a while, the hole was plugged, and the radiation was decontaminated.

The medical pod quickly begins decontamination of the radiation within her body. It has already decontaminated the contaminated compartments of the ship. The computer comes back after the process is complete and says, "There is liver damage. It was repaired as much as it could be repaired, but liver function is down to twenty percent."

That's when Glyria asks, "How long do I have?"

The analyzing computer says, "It is hard to estimate, but with an artificial liver, you can have as long as ten heaps."

After Glyria found out about the captain's death, she was reluctant to tell the truth about her relationship with the captain, and now that she is dying also, she has no reason at all to tell anyone, especially since the captain is dead. She thinks to herself, "If I make it to a new home planet, I will tell his daughter how I really felt about him, and her, too."

Dr. Glyria, after being analyzed and decontaminated, says she feels a whole lot better. After gathering her sources together and beginning to study the planets, they get a team of scientific engineers together and begin to repair the main computer. After all the contaminated parts are replaced and the team gets through fixing the main computer, the computer starts analyzing the ship and all of its components, quickly utilizing people to fix the damaged components.

After three sectors, everything is back to normal, and everybody has their job. Except the navigation system cannot be repaired. It is stuck on a collision course into the center of the sun. The heat source of the sun in its full potential will burn the ship up way before it gets to it. Force fields are reintroduced and engaged for maximum power. This will shield the ship long enough for them to have complete evacuation.

Now each evacuation shuttle has medical facilities, cryogenic facilities, and each one is quite large. With the on board resources, five people can survive up to a heap. Half of that, two heaps, and one person can last up to three or four heaps. Some of the scientists say that survival on these ships could be indefinite, but Dr. Laveman says that has never been tested and he doesn't believe it. He doesn't want to put that theory into action. Although these space ships are large in size, after a heap or two, it would psychologically change a person. "But," he thinks to himself, "anything is possible."

With this on his mind, he concentrates on the planets, and they begin to send out probes to find out more about them. The third planet does not rotate, but it goes around its sun at a very slow pace. It just so happens that the ship is passing behind the planet, blocking its sun source, and they have about a rest before it reaches the other side of the planet to where the ship is going to be in full strength of the sun. After another spot goes by, the front of the ship is coming into the sunlight. It is white hot!

The first planet is just a fireball, a ball of lava. They are not able to establish a rotation report on this planet or determine if it even has a rotation. The second planet, like unto the first, except it has a dark glow on the back. It is half the size of the third planet. It spins in a complete circle every three quarters of a sector. The third planet is the biggest in the solar system. One side is bright orange with a ring of dark around it, and the backside is white. It doesn't rotate, so it is the last to be observed in depth.

The fourth planet rotates two different ways. It spins both around its equator and end over end from its two poles. The way it spins between its two poles is every sector and a half, and around its equator, every six rests. It is only a fourth size of the third planet, about twenty five thousand miles around its circumference on the equator. It is a lot farther away. It is a shimmering blue planet. Were it not for the poisonous gasses on it, it would be the perfect distance away from the sun to maintain life.

The next planet, like unto the rest, gets a little farther away. Some take thousands of heaps to go around the sun. The one farthest away, the twenty-third planet, is the fastest planet of all. It circles the sun every three leans, and it leaves a trail behind it because it moves so fast. You can see the trail for thousands of miles after you are able to view the planet. Its icy trail goes through space leaving a circle halfway around where it travels. After millions of heaps of traveling around, the circle gets bigger around, creating a gravity force field which magnetically pulls space dust into its line of fire. So, when it hits its icy trail coming back around, it penetrates the planet like atomic explosions on its face. It also spins end over end, leaving one side to the sun at all times. Anything caught in its path is destroyed. The circumference around it is about twenty thousand miles, not much smaller than Earth, their predecessor planet.

Nobody here remembers Earth because none of them have ever been there, but thousands of generations have went by since humans left Earth. No one really knows what happened. Some of the data logs are so old and have been manipulated so many times that no one really knows what Earth was like at all. There is a library, but it is hard to tell what is fiction and what is real. When they find a planet, it will be the fourth planet to be colonized. Three planets so far have been destroyed. Resources on the last one were completely abolished. The other two were the same way, also.

They go through each planet. From twenty-three planets down to this last planet, the third one: no life support, no oxygen, toxic gasses, poisons, subzero weather, centrifugal storms, everything from boiling acid to cyanide gasses. They send a probe down to this planet that does not spin. It does not seem to move for the first couple of spots, and then they realize from the telemetry drawn out from the other planets that it does orbit around its sun. But it looks like it is going to take a while, maybe a heap. Being the biggest planet in its solar system, it is red hot on one side with molten lava about four inches thick, and it has subzero weather on the other side.

But in between the two, where the sun isn't directly hitting and the cold isn't directly reflecting, there is a belt around the planet. In certain areas, it stays a warm climate of seventy-five degrees around the belt. But as it goes around the sun, the belt moves around the planet.

To their astonishment and opposite of what they think, the probes come back reporting life. "I don't understand. There's life on this planet," Glyria says. "There should not even be any gravitation."

Dr. Laveman says, "That's impossible! Nothing can live under those kind of conditions."

"But look at these readings," Glyria says. "The probe went to where there is paradise, it seems. There is plant life. There are trees, animals, but it is like the animals are moving constantly. There is also suitable gravitation."

Dr. Laveman says, "The planet does not even turn. How is that possible?"

"There appears to be some magnetic force close to the surface of the planet."

That's when Dr. Tamia, another scientist on their team, says, "I have a theory about this particular rock. It is in one of my logs."

Dr. Laveman says, "Yes, I have read about your theory. It is all hypothetical. At least, it was until now. I've got a feeling you will be looking into that more."

"Yes, sir. I sure will," she replies.

After further study, they find out this planet is inhabitable. Dr. Glyria says, "It looks like the only way we could live on this planet is to be on the move, walking with it heap round fast enough to keep from getting caught in the hot scorching lava part. But if we move too fast, we'll be caught in the subzero freezing weather."

"Well, that's it, then. We have no choice. There is not another option here. Each ship is equipped with a land rover that will withstand a lot of weather but not scorching heat or subzero weather for long, but there is no choice," Dr. Laveman says.

As the other scientists and the command are called to a meeting, they all come to the conclusion that this is the most suitable planet, being how they have nowhere else to go.

Chapter 3
Flashing Before Their Eyes

Two more sectors have gone by, and this massive station, the Planeterial, is now tipping the atmosphere of the belt of this planet. The sun of the solar system has begun to heat up the station. By the hundreds, they enter into the escape shuttles. Each ship is able to fly and land on heavy gravity planets. Once landed, they are able to land rover and move on rocky terrain. The ships leave the Planeterial space station one by one, and as soon as they leave, they get behind the station to where the scorching sun will not burn them up. The front of the station is already on fire. As soon as the station gets into the pathway of the planet, the escape shuttles get into the shadow between the planet and the sun.

There are about five hundred ships. Each one is equipped to hold two to five people. There are families on the station, but they have no more than five members. Every ship has to have at least two people on it. Navigation for each ship was planned and coursed out by the scientists prior to the evacuation. They came to the conclusion before they left that the paradise belt is their only life line, if they are even able to live on this planet at all.

One by one, they enter into the atmosphere, heading for this paradise belt. As the last couple of hundred ships leave the station, the enormous infernal heat of this sun burns the station up. It explodes, taking out about one hundred of the ships. The scorching heat of the sun burns up another hundred or so shuttles, taking out most of the scientists, along with Dr. Glyria, Dr. Lavemen, the second commander, and Captain Sortman.

The last ship witnesses the horrible explosions as one by one, those beside them perish, turning into nothing more than space dust. Some of the nuclear fusion engines make an atomic explosion out of some of the ships. Dorn Bevly is one of the scientists that lives as he witnesses this extraordinary event. When he sees the massive atomic explosions, he can barely see the space station as he sees a light flicker out from the side of it. Then he sees the space station flicker, and then it disappears. The Planeterial is gone. There is nothing left.

Now, Dorn is with two other scientists. One is his sweetheart and has been since they were teenagers. All they can do is cry as they see the ships destroyed and the horrible tragic end of the space station. Neither one of the three think they will survive the landing on the new planet. No one gave much hope when they left the Planeterial.

Newie is Dorn's girlfriend's name, and she is the smartest among the three. Under normal circumstances, she is a little bit abrupt and quite to the point. She runs the show, so to speak, and in her field, she is second to none. She is a nuclear physicist and has quite a bit of pride about it.

Dorn has established a relationship with Newie mainly because she adores him. Although she is a control addict of some sort, even after she tells Dorn what to do, she always asks his opinion about it, and as usual, he will smile and say, "I think that's a great idea." Her eyes will always get big, never knowing what to expect but always getting the same answer, the sweet loving look and the attention she always yearns for from Dorn.

Ledy Night is the other scientist, and she begins to shake from

27

head to toe as she sits with her hands on her face with her arms and head tucked between her legs. Ledy makes sure the computer has analog video of everything that happens including the disappearance of the space station. But not seeing the direct sunlight and seeing the sky get bright the way it does, they can only assume that the sun's gravity had gotten a hold of the station, and all its nuclear fusion and atomic reactors went white hot. That's when they saw the overall bright white light outside of the planet's edges. Even though it only lasts a second, they know there is no going back to what once was, the Planeterial.

Now Dorn is a nuclear physicist, also, but somehow he mixed it with laser technology and is one of the young men that worked with Dr. Laveman on one of the main ship's engines, which is now installed on every shuttle or small space ship.

The shuttles are actually not small at all. The smallest of them all on the inside is thirty-five feet wide, seventy-five feet long, and anywhere from thirty to forty-five feet tall if landed upright. There are three levels on each ship. They are also three corridors wide.

The upper left hand corners of the bottom three on the right have a six feet round tube-like corridor that runs the full length of the ship. There are two ways into each room. If there is gravity, there is a ladder way that leads up into the upper rooms. If there is no gravity, then you just pull yourself along the tube-like corridor and push yourself into whatever room you need to go into. There is also another tube on the upper left side of the ship.

Now the captain's escape shuttle is much bigger, almost three times the size and way more elaborate with more facilities on it, as if the others were not elaborate enough. Radio communications on the captain's shuttle were not functioning at all after the gamma blasts, and neither were network hook-ups for the shuttle to be programmed for the navigation to the location of landing on the new planet. They didn't think to examine all the shuttles since the radiation didn't seem to pass that way. Something else must have happened. After the captain and the crew examined the space shuttle, they realized that they couldn't use it at all. They went into the next escape shuttle which was smaller in size.

Theese Alexander is a family man with a long line of ancestors who can be traced back to Earth. His pod was one of those they believed had malfunctioned. They thought he was deceased. Apparently, the computer had given the wrong analysis of his cryo-pod. He is the first commander of the space station and was in hibernation. After all the escape shuttles blast off, the commander is awakened and de-cryogenilized.

When the commander is fully awake, he realizes that he is alone, all by himself, and that the station is being destroyed. "Quick, Computer, help me! What do I do?!?"

The computer analyzes the situation quickly and assesses that the captain's escape shuttle is the only shuttle left. The navigation to the new planet was stuck into all the computers prior to the evacuation, including the captain's shuttle, at least that's what they thought. "Radio communications for the captain's space shuttle have been eradicated and need extreme repairs. But it is your only hope," the computer tells Commander Alexander.

"Will I get free from this source of destruction?" he asks.

"The chances of survival are seventeen hundred to one," the computer replies.

"So my chances are good, then?"

"Seventeen hundred to one that you will not survive."

"Well, that's not very good!"

The commander runs as quickly as he can back to the space shuttle. "Quickly, locate my family," he demands the computer.

"All remaining passengers have been evacuated from the ship. You are the last one on the vessel. I am afraid the only way to clear any of this is to blast out of the orbit of this solar system. It will put you into light speed."

"There is no telling where I will end up then. I will be by myself," the commander says.

"This is the one chance of your survival," the computer says. "Otherwise, you will perish."

As he straps himself in, the computer energizes all warp and blast off capabilities. As soon as his shuttle de-docks from the space station, it goes into warp.

Now one of the first ships to arrive on the planet carries the young couple, Dr. Sparks and Julia. They are scared of what is ahead and have no idea what to expect. Right at the edge of the cold on the side that enters into the heat, they go down where a bunch of cliffs are. Everything is smooth sailing. The ship is coming up on a soft piece of ground that is flat and level. And as it does, they are happy that they make it.

Three or four more ships just like theirs land in the same area. Each ship was navigated to land approximately five hundred yards away from one another. As they are looking out the window at the other shuttles they can see, they see the rockets turn off one of them. As soon as they turn off, they see the shuttle tilt then sink and disappear into the ground. When one of the other shuttles sees this, they try to take off. They fire the rockets, but it is too late. They tilt, and the rockets are extinguished. They sink the same way.

Sparks and Julia struggle among themselves, wondering what is going to happen to them as other shuttles come and land near the same place. They are sure they are going to perish. While they wait to sink down into the ground, much to their surprise, they don't. Their vessel turns into a land rover. This land rover is equipped with tracks to roll on smooth ground, and it also has extending arms which will climb rocky terrain. So, it is able to go over any part of the land with no problem.

Meanwhile, other ships land on the closer side of the heat where the planet is going into the hot sun. When they land, it is too hot for the shuttles to manipulate their robotics, so they cannot turn into land rovers. About twenty or so ships do the same thing. They literally have a couple of rests before they have full penetration of the hot sun. Although they can live in the shuttles before the heat gets to them, the outside of the shuttles is destroyed. Their ships are doomed!

On the other side of the planet, up toward the mid-north, many of the ships land on this side, too. Those that land in the middle of the belt are safe. Not as many ships perish on this side. It is actually the side that the station could see and plainly lay out the course of navigation for the ships. The other side, they had no idea what was on the rocky terrain which made it more difficult to navigate to. Another fifty or so ships perish in the landing.

There are five scientific engineers in one of the ships, one by the name of Que Bounty. Another one is a beautiful young lady named Serena Silverman. Among these, also, is Fleece Charidon. Now during the landing, they see that they are landing in a clear spot. There are two ships in sight that have already landed. Now, their ship lands. Everybody feels at ease at first, but after a few seconds, the ship begins to go down into the ground. Everybody becomes horrified.

Ms. Silverman, being the first one to look out the window at this particular time as the ship begins to shake and tilt, begins to scream, "We are sinking! Quickly, do something!" By this time, the window panes are covered with darkness.

On another ship, Tarvin Dasin wakes groggily to the sound of alarms blaring and red lights flashing through his burred vision. Gaping holes in the vessel expose him to the planet's atmosphere. His copilot's seat is still held in place, but the ship has landed at an angle. He struggles to breathe as his vision clears up a little. He undoes his restraints and falls from his seat, his head pounding painfully. The ship's view screen is completely gone along with the pilot's seat and the pilot. Memories of what happened come trickling back to him as he stumbles to the door and pulls a lever down to open the door.

"Error," the computer says. "Hull breach. Atmosphere not regulated."

"Overide," Tarvin says, groaning as his head pounds painfully.

"Overide comfirmed," the computer's monotone voice answers as the door slides halfway open and loses power.

Tarvin squeezes through the gap in the doorway, only to see another scene of destruction. The side of the ship has been completely torn off. Wires, strewn across the floor, are sparking. The hull is dented and bent out of shape in several places. He can feel a slight breeze coming through.

Tarvin doesn't even try to consider the situation they are in as he hurries over to his sister who is still strapped to the passenger's seat. He feels relief course through him as he grabs her wrist and feels a pulse. She is unconscious, bruised, and bloody, the same as he is, but they appear to be only minor injuries. Ignoring the pain in his body, he undoes her restraints and lets her down as gently as he can, the awkward position of the ship making this difficult.

Tarvin quickly grabs the only remaining life support helmet

and puts it on her. As he does this, her breathing evens out. The atmosphere is obviously breathable, or he would be dead, but he is still struggling to breathe. His body will need time to adapt to the different oxygen levels.

That's when he quickly stands as he hears a scream followed by loud sobs. He hurries to the ladder leading down into the medical bay. He slides down the ladder to find that the medical bay is still partially intact although there are still many holes in the vessel.

A woman whom Tarvin immediately recognizes as Dr. Sora Holis is kneeling over a man, sobbing loudly and gripping his hand tightly. Tarvin steps forward hesitantly. "Dr Holis..."

She turns toward him, tears pouring down her face and pleading in her eyes. "Please!" she begs. "Help him!" Then she bursts into another fit of sobbing.

Tarvin kneels down beside him, doing his best to ignore the blood. He isn't a doctor, but he doesn't have to be. The moment he had seen the large piece of shrapnel in the man's chest, he had known there was nothing he could do for him. He is already dead, eyes staring lifelessly up at him.

Each of their suits have their names on them, and the man's suit reads the same as the woman's, "Dr. Hollis." Tarvin realizes they are married. They had been in a rush to leave the Planeterial and had not had time for proper introductions. Tarvin had not even known the pilot of the ship, and he was the co-pilot. The only person he knew on board was his sister, Iniria Dasin. But he remembers helping Dr. Hollis when his cryo-pod malfunctioned on board the space station.

"I'm sorry," Tarvin says as he reaches over and closes the man's eyes. He stands abruptly and leaves Dr. Hollis where she is, still sobbing violently.

He goes back to the ladder and climbs back up to where his

sister is beginning to wake up. "It's alright. I'm here," he says soothingly as he kneels down beside her.

She hugs him, and he hugs her back. Iniria is only twelve heaps old but has an IQ greater than most people, including Tarvin. "Are you okay?" he asks when she finally lets go.

"I think so," she says, shaking her head yes.

"Okay, I'm going to check the ship's systems. Why don't you stay here and see if you can salvage anything?"

Iniria nods, and Tarvin's thoughts turn to Dr. Holis' body as he decides that she definitely shouldn't see that. He doesn't want to frighten her anymore than she probably already is. "We're going to be alright," Tarvin says, smiling encouragingly at her as he stands, and he is relieved to get a smile back.

Only around two hundred fifty ships make it, mostly families. The death of the other two hundred and fifty ships include those that are going to perish going into the cold of this harsh planeterial environment and those going into the heat because their ships are not able to convert into land rovers. A couple of the ships are not able to convert when they land too close to the cold side of the belt due to some of the ships being damaged during the landing. But once the orbit of the new world gets to where they are in the paradise belt where it warms up, their vehicles do convert, and they are able to land rover and stay in the good climate.

Although frightened of the environment of a hostile planet, Sparks and Julia want to investigate, so they establish communication between the ships. Radio communication is possible, but it does not carry very far. Those in the north on the planet relay the messages from those in the south of the planet but not too far south. Radio communication only goes a few miles, but they are able to establish a link between the vehicles and begin trying to gather the information of how many people actually survived.

Among the first they communicate with is Doc Husby. Now Mr. Husby was one of the oldest living family men upon the station. He has an older son about the age of twenty-three, and his younger daughter is eighteen. His wife is a little younger than he is. She is some type of school teacher. They have just had a young boy not too many heaps before they went into cryogenics. He is almost seven heaps old.

Everything the young boy has experienced up to this point is exciting and, to say the least, a blast. He keeps saying, "This is great!"

The ship is torn to and fro. There are sirens going off, explosions. You would think he is at a playground or something. Because of his youth, he does not realize the seriousness of it all, and his parents do not lead him to believe otherwise.

Now, little Brittle is the first to hear radio communications. He calls for his dad, terribly excited. That's when they hear Sparks on communications, saying, "Does anybody hear me?"

Mr. Husby says, "This is Doc Husby. Who is this?"

"This is Dr. Sparks and my wife, Julia. Are ya'll okay?"

"A little banged up and shook up, but otherwise, everything seems to be intact, including communications. It is really good to hear from you."

That's when the air becomes full of voices. "We're okay, too. We are the Leevman family." One after another, as far as radio communications will reach, each family communicates with the others.

That's when Sparks hears it. It sounds like an atomic explosion. One of the ships that went down close to the cliff landed too close to the edge, and before they could get leveled out, the ledge gave way. The ship went crashing to the bottom. That's when the nuclear fusion pods busted open, and the fuselage busted open, also. When the fuselage lit up, it created enough explosion to rupture the inner core of the nuclear fusion pod. When it did, six ships were taken out. It lit up the whole sky!

Sparks grabs a hold of anything he can grab a hold of as the ship shakes violently. At first, he thinks the planet is blowing up. But after a few short moments, he realizes that something must have really went wrong with one of the ships. One of the families they had been communicating with does not respond afterward, and after that, several others.

Doc Husby is the first out after the blast and realizes that nobody can get close enough except for those in the space suits. Now the space suits are designed to shield off radioactivity, especially nuclear radiation such as plutonium gives out. The data transfer from the six ships that were destroyed was instantly transferred to all the ship's computers, but Doc Husby's ship was the closest and the only one that could receive it before he transferred it to other ships.

After examining the blast, he sees that there is nothing left of the cliff, and there is a half a mile crater where the ship was. Being five hundred yards from the original blast, the force field of the other ships kept the nuclear blast from blowing them up also, but everyone on board was destroyed as their ships were picked up off the ground and slung through the air like lava from a volcano.

After Doc goes to each ship and realizes that everybody on board is dead, he goes back to his own ship and relays what happened as he reads the data that was transferred to his ship. The last entry says that the fuselage was ruptured. Before that, the nuclear fusion reactor was ruptured also, which undoubtedly caused the explosion from the beginning.

Meanwhile, on the lower side of the northern part of the planet, there are three ships that land. Three scientists, elderly gentlemen in their fifties, two scientists in another ship in their early forties, and another scientist and his family of four, two sons, teenagers that are very, very educated, above average geniuses, Ronson and his brother, Corton. Although Corton is smaller in stature and younger, he is the more intelligent one, his IQ almost doubling his brother's. No matter how smart Ronson imposes, his little brother always makes him sound smarter. They are always adding to each other. The three elder scientists are also geniuses. After establishing communication with the others, they believe there are not more than twenty or so scientists left alive with this massive IQ level.

One of the last ships to land is Dorn, Newie, and Ledy's ship. The ship automatically navigates to a small clearing. It is just big enough. Perfect landing! Everything is smooth and operational. The robotic arms quickly extend out, and from underneath the ship, four sets of tracks with two tracks on each side of each one with six feet wheels on the inside of them extend out. Minimum leveling is needed, and gravitation is suitable.

After checking the atmosphere and the air with an electronic probe on the outside of the ship, the computer comes back online and says, "All atmosphere and air is suitable for life support, including rich oxygen."

There are two ways off the ship. One is a ladder way that extends down to the ground up to thirty feet. The other is an extending elevator that comes out from the bottom with an electronic arm. It is nothing more than a platform that extends down to the ground. It can also move throughout the bottom of the ship, enabling repairs if necessary.

Dr. Bevly puts his space suit on, carrying his helmet in his hand just in case of emergencies. The hatch opens. The rich oxygen-filled air fills up the compartment where he is along with Newie and Ledy. They stay behind, waiting patiently for Dr. Bevly to step down the ladder. As he walks out about thirty or forty feet from the ladder way, that's when Newie starts to step down onto the ladder.

Dorn turns around just in time as the planet shakes violently. He looks at Newie as she holds onto the ladder. Then, a split opens up about forty or fifty feet long. It comes right underneath the ladder where Newic is. At the beginning of the split, hot atmosphere comes spewing up about seventy-five feet. Dr. Bevly stands there in shock as it heads down the opening to where Newie is.

She turns and looks at him, and all she can think is, "How is Dorn going to be without me?" Knowing how much he loves her, even facing death, she can think of nothing but his happiness. As the hot atmosphere hits the ladder, it singes the ladder with hot debris as it sends Newie sailing through the air.

Ledy, on the inside, is blown to the back of the corridor. She is severely injured with a broken arm and a fractured leg. That's when Newie lands about fifty feet on the other side of the ship. Dr. Dorn Bevly stands there in shock as he watches Newie fly in the air. His heart sinks to the ground. All he can do is fall to his knees, and as the planet opens up, it closes back in the same manner. The only harm to the ship is the ladder itself where it is singed.

Ledy pulls herself to the opening as she looks at Dorn. She loves him intensely and has nothing but respect for his love for Newie. She loves Newie, also, and knows how much they mean to each other. But when she sees him in a kneeled down position with his eyes open wide and his mouth dropped, she busts out crying. She can feel nothing but his pain, not even giving second thought

38

to her broken arm and fractured leg.

She cries with a loud voice, "Dorn! Are you okay?!?" He is speechless. "Dorn, are you okay?!?" she yells again.

All he can do is look at her and shake his head a little bit up and down, weakened by the sudden event that just happened before him. He slowly comes up from a kneel to his feet and walks to the other side of the ship. There she lays. She is broken from one end to the other, her face scarred and burned. Half her hair has been blown away from the blast. Her eyes are wide open as he remembers her looking into his eyes.

He says, "I love you, my dear." And then he puts his hands on her eyes and closes them. He busts out crying with a loud howl, groaning with an unquenchable groan, a pain like no one has ever heard. Ledy, not being able to come to him, can hear him from the other side of the ship. She begins to groan too for the loss she knows her best friend is feeling and for her dearest companion who is perished.

Dorn picks Newie's broken body up, carries her back to the front not too far from where the door is open on the ship, and lays her down. As he kneels down beside her and groans really loud one more time, he begins to cry.

By this time, Ledy makes her way to the elevator. With a fractured leg and a broken arm, she wings her way to Dr. Bevly. As she comes upon him sobbing, she grabs him and holds him tight. She busts out crying again, feeling nothing but pain in her chest. She can hardly hold in the emotion as she takes her hand and pulls his face around to hers. She shakes her head backward and forward and says to him, "I'm so sorry." She pulls his head close to her and holds him tight as she sobs one last time then faints from the pain.

When Dorn sees Ledy pass out on the ground, he realizes that her injuries are more serious than she let on. He quickly picks her up and shakes off the pain and anguish of the death of his love. As he reaches the platform to be elevated back up to the ship, in fear of the ground opening back up again, he makes haste and quickly gets into the ship.

On entry, she wakes up, not knowing where she is or what happened. She says, "What happened?"

"Apparently you have several injuries. I'm putting you into the medical pod."

As he slides her into the medical pod, the computer quickly analyzes a broken leg, two fractured ribs, a broken arm in two different places, a slight concussion, and two broken fingers, her pinky and her last finger on her left hand. As the computer tells him all the injuries she has, he says, "Computer, that's impossible. She walked to me from the ship, almost a hundred feet."

The computer comes back and says, "Due to cryogenics, adrenaline, and the shock of losing her best friend, she probably could have climbed a mountain and not realized it."

Now Dorn has no little love for Ledy. He loves her just as he did Newie but not in exactly the same way, but his already protective manner for Newie will triple for Ledy now that Newie is dead.

Although two hundred and something ships perish in the fire, explosions, and hostile planet environment, over two hundred and fifty survive. It ends up to be about eleven hundred people. Unfortunately, four hundred or so perish. They reason among themselves, saying it was no better to leave the planet that they left from. They say were doomed to die there, and now they are doomed to die here, too. Only they don't know it but the planet is no longer there anymore. Neither is the solar system. This is the third time they have tried to re-establish planeterial homes, being how the solar system of the natural Earth's sun burnt out. This is now the third solar system, and it is not the one they were heading for. It had taken hundreds of heaps to build a space station, and now they figure it will take a hundred more to figure out how to build another space station without it melting in the gamma blasting sun.

Chapter 4
Help Me Live

Before heading back to the front of the ship, Tarvin removes a tool kit from a storage compartment in the wall, then he squeezes back through the door, realizing as he does so how dangerous this is. If at any time the ship's power decides to come back on, the door will either continue to open or it will seal shut once more, and he definitely doesn't want to be in between it if that happens.

Before going over to the console, he walks over to the large gap in the ship and stands awe struck as he gets his first good look at the planet's surface. There are no clouds. The sky is so clear that you can see the stars and the planets as if you are looking out a view screen in space. The ship has crashed into the side of a mountain, and Tarvin can see for miles. Vibrant colors and plant life like nothing he has ever seen before spread out before him, broken up by jagged mountains and cliffs. It is truly a stunning sight.

Tarvin shakes himself back to reality and turns to the ship's computer console. He takes some tools and removes a panel from the ship. He fiddles with the wiring for a moment and grins as the console comes back to life. "Ship's status?" Tarvin asks as his hands move over the console and the alarms cease, although the lights continue to flash warningly.

"Life support failure, engine failure, hull breach, power failure in..." As the computer continues on, Tarvin grows more and more ill tempered.

"Let me rephrase that question. What is still operational?"

"System check and computer systems still operational. Power in the medical bay and cockpit still operational."

"No kidding, I just fixed that," he says absentmindedly as his mind races. "What about the conversion into a rover?"

"Negative, conversion not possible."

"Figured that," Tarvin thinks to himself. As he picks up his tool kit, he says, "Begin automatic system repair."

"Automatic systems will have minimal effect," the computer warns.

Tarvin nods. "Do what you can. I'll see what I can do on my end." He turns toward the door, but then another thought crosses his mind. "Do you have the data on the planet from the Planeterial?"

"Affirmative."

Tarvin removes his data pad from the tool kit. "Transfer the information to my data pad. I'll take a look at it."

"Affirmative."

Tarvin fixes the door before going through, the ghastly images of it closing on him flashing through his mind. As he tests the door and then walks through, he glances out of one of the gaps, and fear strikes his heart as he sees Iniria outside, standing in a field of thin bluish plant life.

As Tarvin left Iniria to go work on the ship, Iniria wandered over to one of the holes in the vessel, and when she looked out, she was struck by the same amazing sight her brother had seen. She suddenly had the irresistible desire to go outside. She made her way to the back of the ship and released the airlock that led outside. Excitement raced through her, and she held her breath as she took her first step on the planet. The gravity was pretty much what she was used to, and the ground was firm beneath her feet.

She takes a few steps, looking around at the beautiful sights around her when she suddenly feels something latch onto her suit. At fist, she is confused as she sees nothing, but then the strange bluish plant life she had at first ignored, as it resembled grass or wheat, changes color to a dark red and latches onto her from all sides. Fear grips her as she finds she can't move, and the grass-like plants wrap around her, growing as they do so.

She is about to scream, but she suddenly feels strong arms pick her up, and she hugs Tarvin tightly as the plants unroot themselves from the ground, slither away like snakes, reroot themselves in another patch of blue grass, and mimic their color once again.

Tarvin doesn't put her down until he gets back to the ship, and when he does, he sees that she is crying. "Don't ever do that again, okay?" he says urgently, relieved that she is alright.

Iniria shakes her head yes, too much in shock to speak, and hugs him tightly again.

After Dr. Sora Hollis regains some form of control, they bury Dr. Holis' body while Iniria works on repairing some of the computer systems. As they walk back to the ship, Tarvin speaks. "Doctor...?" he asks awkwardly. He has never been very good at social interaction, especially in emotional situations. "I don't mean to intrude on your grief or anything, but we need to get this ship running..... So...I need to know.... Exactly what do you have a doctorate in?"

She nods, giving him a half smile. "Of course. I'm a psychologist."

Tarvin stops in his tracks as she continues on. "A psychologist....," he mutters as he enters the ship. "Of all the useful doctors I could have crash landed on a planet with, I get the psychologist."

After he checks on Iniria to find that she is in her quarters sleeping peacefully, he takes his data pad and leaves the ship, finding a rock which he can sit on and glancing at the sky which hasn't changed since they landed. He powers up the data pad and finds the information about the planet which he scrolls through, his mood darkening by the moment. "Computer, analyze the planet's orbit, and pinpoint our location," he tells the data pad which is remotely connected to the ship's computer.

An image of the planet appears on the screen followed by a red arrow pinpointing their location on the planet. Evidently they have landed somewhere in the southern hemisphere. Tarvin has no idea if any of the other ships have survived, and after the rough landing they had, he doesn't keep his hopes up.

"Adjust visual to infrared." That's when the image changes, and Tarvin realizes just how difficult their survival has become. Because of the planet's orbit around the sun, half of the planet is a frozen wasteland while the other half is a burning inferno. Only a relatively small ring around the planet is inhabitable, but that isn't the real problem. The paradise belt, which Tarvin later discovers it is called, moves constantly. So, the planet is constantly being burned and then refrozen. So, each time the planet makes a full orbit, the scenery and life on the planet change. The only way to survive here is to move with the planet, which with their ship in its current condition is impossible.

"Computer, give me a timetable," Tarvin says as he considers all this. Numbers appear on the screen that slowly count down. "So, about forty-eight spots before the heat becomes too much for us to handle," he thinks, rounding the numbers, "which means we need to have the ship up and running within thirty-nine spots."

Now even as he thinks this, he knows it is hopeless. It hadn't taken him long to discover that the shuttle would never fly again.

He ponders on this for a while, and unable to come up with a suitable solution for the amount of time they have, he finally returns to the ship and falls asleep.

Meanwhile, underground, Dr. Charidon grabs Serena and says, "Look, it will be okay! We are not gonna die!"

"What do you mean we are not gonna die?"

"Well, we are gonna die eventually, but I mean just not right yet. We are in a space ship. We can live indefinitely with the resources on board. It will be okay. We will figure this out," he tells her. She takes in a sobering breath and shakes her head as they sit back down in their seats and fasten their seat belts.

After several moments of sinking, they finally hit what they think is the bottom of the sinking terrain. These sinking spots are all over the planet. It is the only soil that does not crystallize in the hot scorching heat and does not freeze in the freezing cold terrain of the dark side. The vessel finally lands at a tilt. That's when the computer uses the robotic arms and levels out the ship. The computer comes on and says, "The ship is leveled, and all systems are operational."

Each ship is equipped with five life pods. Cryogenics are included with these life pods along with emergency procedures and other things. After analyzing what is happening, two of the scientists decide they want to go back into cryogenics while the other three figure out how to get out of the mess they are in. That's when Fleece says, "That's it. Ya'll are just going to go back to sleep?!?"

One is a very young woman. She puts her hands on his chest and says, "We're not worried. We have full assurance ya'll will get us out of this mess."

They both climb back into their pods and go into cryogenics as their pods are sucked back into the wall. That's when Serena says, "Well, is there anybody else going to go to sleep? Can you believe those guys? Wake them, if we need them...What a mess we are in!"

Que shakes his head, realizing that she is in shock, and tells her, "If I wasn't needed, I would go to sleep, too, to save the resources on the ship. Maybe you ought to go to sleep, too."

"Cryogenics?!? In a time like this?" Serena says. "I'm sorry, Que, but I would like to stay awake if that's okay." After this sobering thought, Serena quickly pulls herself together and gets busy about saving their lives.

Now everyone on the Planeterial has scientific degrees, doctor's degrees, and each person was chosen for a particular duty which was reserved for them by those higher up in the chain from the captain on down. These five scientists are very smart and extremely adequate. Mr. Charidon is more than just an engineer. He is the one that designed the electrical impulse engine. He is also one of the three that designed the blue metal fusion energy, the metal of which was found off the moon of one of the planets in the Sherayus galaxy, which gives off a pure natural energy used mostly in low voltage. Although it is continuous energy, it is not extremely powerful but is extremely useful.

Que is six feet, nine inches tall, a very tall gentleman, very masculine, and kinda snobbish, to say the least. Like for instance, one spot soon after they sink, Serena is coming through one of the walkways when Que is walking out. She stops right in the way, and he says, "Are you coming in or out? Or are you just going to stand there?"

She looks at him and says, "No, I'm coming in."

Now Serena, on the norm, is a very, very wonderful person. She overlooks Que's ways and just attributes them to the circumstances they are in. But inwardly, she seeks desperately to find his approval which she obviously does not have which draws her to seek approval even more.

After Que walks out, she runs into Fleece, and he says to her, "Can you believe that guy?"

"What do you mean?" she asks.

"Well, I just think he could be a little nicer. That's all."

"Oh, he's just under a little stress," she tells him.

"Who wouldn't be? Look where we're at. We're at the bottom of some kinda … I don't even know what this stuff is. But I've got an idea to get us out of here. The only bad thing is that if we're not on the bottom, it could prove to be worse than where we are. But the robotic arms on the ship are strong enough to move us about on the bottom here." After he expounds on his plan, they all agree that the robotic arms will walk them off to the edge. So, the robotic arms begin to walk. They move the ship approximately six inches.

That's when Que says, "Oh great, at this rate, we might be here another twenty heaps."

The computer says, "On the contrary, only approximately eight heaps."

"Only eight heaps?!? Really?!? ONLY eight heaps?!?"

The computer comes back and says, "If the tracks would touch the ground and rotate, which they will not, it would take less time. Unfortunately, the tracks are clogged with the material that we are unable to analyze at this particular time, so it will be eight heaps before it reaches the surface."

On the surface of the planet, Sparks and Julia are now wanting to test the environment. They decide they are going to step out after watching plants and animals of all sizes and shapes through the window. They notice there is an area about the size of the captain's ship which was left on the Planeterial, about a hundred yards, where plants and animals don't grow or go. After observing this, they realize that these are sinking pods on the ground. Anything that walks over them, after a few seconds or so, will sink like lead in water. Talk about a death trap.

After two rests of studying the environment, taking atmosphere readings, and taking robotic moisture readings, they realize that the air is much cleaner than their previous planet's air, and the oxygen is much richer. They step out in life support suits, space suits as we call them today, and Sparks is the first one to take off his helmet. He takes in a deep breath, and a certain burst of energy comes over him. With an extreme amount of enthusiasm, he says, "Yeah! I can breathe! It's great! Come on, Julia! It's like an exhilarating fresh breath of air!"

The smell in the air is sweet. There is a soft breeze that blows constantly but never more than four miles per sector, which is less than one mile a quarter sector. It always blows toward the warm side but is never harsh. There is no rain, and it stays light seven sectors a spot. If you travel too fast toward the cold, it gets a little dimmer, and if you stay put in one area too long, after a few rests, it will get lighter and lighter. This is a warning. The lighter it gets, the hotter it gets. The hotter it gets, the closer to the sun's light you are getting. You cannot get in direct sunlight ever. You have to be in a sun down position constantly on this planet to be outside. If you get caught in the sunlight, you perish. If you get caught in the dark, you perish, depending on what side of the planet you are on.

You can be at the northern hemisphere of the paradise belt or the southern hemisphere. You can be directly north or directly south. Sparks and Julia are on the northern hemisphere on the side that goes into the sun if you stand still. There are people on the other side of the northern hemisphere in the belt. If they stand still, they will go into the ice and cold. But later they find that you can spend about six leans at the northern hemisphere because it stays warm without getting cold, and you can actually establish plant life and raise livestock.

Communication with each ship, north and south pole of the new planet, has been well established. With the help of Corton, Ronson, and the others, they quickly establish the fact that they will have to move every three leans until they get near the top where there is no ice at all. Although you can't live directly at the north pole, near there, you can stay for nine leans without picking up and moving completely off. They have to travel three leans to stay in one place nine leans, or those at a lower position, they can travel one rest out of each four rests. This north pole and the south pole are valuable. The object of the game is to travel until you can't take the cold anymore, stay there until you can't take the heat, and then move.

Most of the ships are able to gather together in a hundred mile radius at the nine lean point. This is the cold part of the heap. After all the families, leaders, scientists, and doctors get together...all the scientists are doctors, but not all the doctors are scientists... everybody is assigned a part, and nobody does anything they don't want to do. It is all a joint effort. It has to be this way unless they want to depend on the ships that may or may not last, and if they do, it certainly will not be generational.

Now, Ronson and his brother come up with idea with some charter and navigational equipment that it will be better to look for another solar system. Now Corton, being the smarter one, realizes that they only have nine leans to build a vessel, get it into space, and keep it on the dark side of the planet until they can actually build onto it big enough to establish another space station. This is going to take an extreme amount of engineering.

The sun has a solar storm one spot, and communication with the south pole, the ships down there, is able to be clearly understood for about four sectors. This is when they realize that more than twenty of the scientists are alive. Altogether, there are about eleven hundred people that survived, but it takes a while to establish this information. Nobody knows exactly who perished and how many perished because they never established the correct number of people or vessels before they left. Some of the scientists knew they had five hundred ships, and that is what they know about.

Meanwhile, colonization is on its way, eleven hundred or so survivors colonizing a planet with hostile plants, animals, and all kinds of vegetation. It is no time at all before they have crops up and going from seeds they had saved from the prior planet they left. The good thing about colonizing the planet is that when you plant a seed, the other seeds take its environment and mimic it. If you plant corn, it grows corn, and it grows it very fast. In a couple of rests, you have a corn crop. It doesn't grow very many corn on the stalks, but they are very big and very good. If you grow a tomato plant, you are liable to get three tomatoes, but it will be three of the best tomatoes there has ever been. And they quickly reproduce after they are picked.

Each ship carried a little bit of livestock that was put into stasis to be woke up and readmitted into reproduction. Power cells, solar cells, and cold fusion cells are a part of every ship, a limitless supply of energy in three astronomical ways. Each ship is equipped with waste recycling for water and food. If nothing goes wrong with the ship itself, you can live on it indefinitely, theoretically.

Unfortunately, they find that some of the plant life is more hostile than the sun's heat on surface of the planet. One spot,

Sparks is visiting one of the other ships with a family of five on it. They are all in their space suits and afraid to take their suits off. Although Sparks encourages them to do so, the dad will not allow it. It is a good thing that they don't because while they are outside visiting with Sparks and Julia, one of the tree-like plants lifts up its roots out of the ground, flies thirty feet up in the air and two hundred feet over to where the ship is, opens up its leaf-like mouth, and consumes the whole ship like it is a blanket over it. Then, it takes it roots and sticks them back in the ground, never moving the ship from its origin.

With no ship to stay on, Sparks leads them back to his ship. After a half of a sector of investigating and fellowshipping, they all have to take rest. Upon awakening, they go back outside to look at plant life they have started cultivating. When they do, they look over to where the ship was. They see that the plant-like animal that ate it realized it could not digest it and left it where it was with about a foot of slime all over it. The plant-like animal is nowhere in sight. It has disappeared. It has apparently flown off or worse.

Sparks looks at Mr. Malantium and says, "Well, you still have your home, even though it is pretty well slimed. We had better run some analysis on this slime to make sure it is safe." They go back to Sparks' ship to get some lab equipment to run some tests, and by the time they get back, the gooey-like slime has ran off and been absorbed by the ground.

They think all the plant-like animals are all deadly, but they soon find other uses for them. One spot, while Sparks and Julia are planting more seeds, Sparks steps into a hole. His foot is stuck. Others rush to help him, but meanwhile, a big plant-like animal flies down beside him, swallowing him and the hole his foot is stuck in, ground and all.

Julia freezes in shock. She and Sparks were not married long before they were stuck in cryogenics. They knew each other before then about a heap, but they are all each other have. When she sees Sparks disappear into the mouth of this plant-like animal, then sees it leave root from the ground and fly off, it is as though her life falls from her body. She falls lifelessly to the ground on her knees. It is as though she does not want to live any longer.

Three quarters of a sector later, Mr. Malantium gets word over the radio that a plant-like animal landed thirty feet from a vessel, spit a man out, then turned white as snow and perished. When he goes to investigate, he realizes it is Sparks. He quickly begins to wipe the goo off him while the ground soaks it up from one side, and what he knocks off, it quickly soaks up.

Sparks is throwing up all kinds of goo as he sucks in air by the lungs full. He quickly says, "I didn't need to breathe. Until I spit that stuff out. Whatever it is, it is full of oxygen."

He relays this information on to Ronson and his brother, which proves to be valuable information later on. Word is sent to Julia that Sparks is alive. Still recovering from the shock at this new found news, she finally bursts out into tears and cries for the first time.

The plant life and animal life on this planet cannot adapt to anything new. The plants have to eat. The animals have to eat. But they can only eat what they have eaten previously. They cannot adapt to a new process of food or it will kill them. The good thing about the plant life is that once one dies, the others know not to venture into where it died at or do the same thing. They learn from each other. They learn quickly in the short season that they live.

Along with other amazing things on the planet, the plant life and plant growth literally happen in a sector of time. The only bad thing is that its life span is not long. After a few leans, everything either goes into the cold and freezes to death, or if it is on the other side, it goes into the heat and burns up. If it doesn't walk and move along the paradise belt, it perishes one way or another. It takes a while to learn all this information, all of which proves valuable.

Sparks makes haste to get home to his wife. As soon as Julia sees him, she runs as hard as she can into his arms and bursts out crying. "I thought you were dead. I thought I would never see you again!" she says.

He says, "You ain't gonna get rid of me that easy."

He quickly expounds, saying, "The craziest thing is that I didn't have to breathe when I was inside of that thing. When I tried to take in a breath, I thought I was going to smother. I choked and took in more of that goo into my lungs. I choked again, and after I sucked in more, my lungs were full of it. I couldn't take in anymore. Then, I blacked out. I woke up a little while afterward, but I didn't have to breathe. My lungs were taking in oxygen through the pores, and the CO_2 was just going out of my mouth with bubbles through the slime that was inside the plant. If a person was to get their lungs full of this stuff, they could probably dive into water very deep without having to breathe. It could be used for all kinds of things: underground, life support on a ship. It has countless versatilities." He makes haste to let the scientists know all this.

Meanwhile, Tarvin spends half the next spot going over their situation with the computer, and by the time he comes up with a solution, he starts to wonder if having a psychologist with them is so useless after all. "What's your analysis?" Tarvin asks the computer, although he already knows the answer after sectors of working on their doomed vessel.

"Analyzing data from ship's systems. Data confirmed. With the current rate of repairs and assuming you are able to accumulate the needed materials, it will take 235.65 spots to make the vessel operational again," the computer says, finally showing some of the personality it has been programmed with. "Considering the amount of time remaining, it would be simpler to build another vessel. Perhaps with smaller dimensions."

"What?" Tarvin asks as hope fills him, and his mind begins to race as ideas begin to come together in his head. "I can do this," he thinks.

"With the curr...." the computer begins again, but Tarvin is way ahead of it.

"Nevermind that," Tarvin says, interrupting the computer as he grabs his data pad and begins to work on a design. It doesn't take him long to work out a design that can be built with the supplies on board and what can be salvaged from their ship, the computer adding occasional input. When Tarvin finally finishes and decides to show the doctor and his sister, his ship resembles no ship that has ever been built. As a matter of fact, it looks more like a half of a ship, and when he shows them, Dr. Holis and Iniria genuinely think he has gone mad. After he begins to explain the design further, they become less skeptical and begin to put in their own ideas. They are soon just as excited as he is.

Iniria particularly enjoys this as her brother is her hero, and even though she has a higher IQ than his mathematically, she knows she could never apply it or improvise the way her brother does, who has already managed to successfully get the various parts of their new vessel running, often using very illogical methods. One method in particular is when he will occasionally hit a stubborn piece of equipment with whatever tool he happens to have in hand. To her great astonishment, it often works, even though it makes no sense whatsoever.

Tarvin, on the other hand, knows he can't do it without her and spends many sleepless spots working on the vessel, the increasing temperature an ever present reminder of the approaching danger. His desire to save his sister pushes him above and beyond the point where many would have broken down. Even though Iniria knows nothing of the coming danger, she senses his urgency and does the best she can to help him, often finding him asleep wherever he has been working. Iniria's intellectual mind also takes notice of the increasing heat, and she suspects danger but makes a point not to interrupt her brother's work with questions unless they are about the vessel or otherwise imperative to their survival.

Tarvin told Dr. Holis about their situation at the beginning and has been relieved to find out that even though her main doctorate is in psychology, she also has several other more useful doctorates that required her to have more technological expertise. As a psychologist, Dr. Holis finds Tarvin and Iniria to be extremely interesting. Both of them are exceptional, especially for their age, but what is really interesting is that even though they are both highly intellectual, they seem to have more of a laid-back personality that isn't common in recent generations. Even though Dr. Holis inevitably spends a lot of time around them, she finds that she doesn't really know what to make of them, and the only refuge she finds from the pain of the death of her husband is in her work.

Finally, the time comes to test the ship. Tarvin holds his data pad in his hand, the heat visible in infrared inching slowly toward the icon that indicates the position of their ship. This is it. This is their last chance. There won't be time for anything else. They are now at seven spots, and the screen continues to count down. The heat has become unbearable.

Tarvin, Iniria, and Dr. Holis step onto their vessel and sit down on the seats Tarvin has installed. "Computer, begin initial start-up sequence." The console in front of Tarvin comes to life as he says this, and Iniria reaches over and squeezes his hand tightly. He can see the complete trust in her eyes.

"Sequence complete," the computer says. "Ready for take off."

"This is it, God," Tarvin thinks in one last desperate plea for help. "Please don't let it end like this!" Then, he presses the button. The vessel rises from the ground about three feet before the engine sputters and then evens out. It works!

"All systems fully operational," the computer says. Tarvin is certain he can detect a tone of relief in the computer's voice, but naturally the computer would deny such a thing.

Chapter 5
Hope for the Future

During colonization, they begin to learn more and more about the planet little by little. Near the northern hemisphere, not far away from the equator, the terrain doesn't change much. Up to this point, this is the biggest planet mapped out of the whole star system. Around its equator is over one hundred thousand miles. There is no way a person can travel around its equator fast enough to stay out of its harsh environment. If you don't live in the northern hemisphere or the southern hemisphere, you will not be able to keep up with its orbit around the sun.

The equator, on the part that is directly in the sun, is twenty five percent molten rock, lava at about four inches thick. Now while that part is in the sun, it causes massive volcanoes. It literally melts everything in its path around the equator. Once it gets cooled off, the rocky terrain is different heap round. It is never the same, never the same mountain, never the same valley.

On the equator going into the sun, there are massive lands of ice. When it warms up and melts, it creates a cloud just on the outside of each side of the equator. When it goes out of the sun, it causes two hundred percent precipitation, massive flooding, massive rain. It is like a literal sheet of water until it stops raining down which in some places cools the lava off and forms new mountains instantly. It will rain until it hits the ice and cools off again. So, this creates a rain forest between the heat and the cold state.

It also creates massive lakes, but once it hits the cold, the lakes will freeze. Every drop of water will freeze all over again until it reaches the other side, goes back into the sun, and evaporates. In that particular area coming out of the sun, the moisture stays at two hundred percent moisture. On the other side, where it melts, there is a continual cloud cover where it stays dark and stormy and precipitates whenever it feels the need if the cloud has not evaporated into the heat of the sun which is later dispersed on the other side.

The weather never changes around the equator. It stays exactly the same. One side it rains. One side it mists. One size is freezing. The other side is hot. There is no way to live anywhere close to the equator. You have to live either in the northern hemisphere or the southern hemisphere. The only way to cross is by ship very swiftly.

Because of this climate, there are new plants, new animals, a new species every few leans around the equator in the paradise belt. Nothing lives outside of the paradise belt. The freezing cold gets two or three hundred degrees below zero. That is moderate weather. At its coldest point, it can reach freezing cold weather of about three hundred degrees freezing. The cold part is only about twenty-five percent of the planet's surface.

Now there is a crack in the surface from the middle of the northern hemisphere to the middle of the southern hemisphere. It is thousands of miles long. Each heap, the crack will go into the lava, evaporating the water out of it. As soon as it gets back around, it will fill up with water until it gets to the other side, then it will evaporate. In some spots, especially in the northern hemisphere, when the water fills the bottom up, it turns into a thick substance called woosh. It is hundreds of miles down, but this keeps massive flooding from the northern hemisphere and southern hemisphere on one side and creates a lot of recreation on the other side.

The volatile state of the planet seems to create a life sustainable, stable part on the rest of the planet but only in certain areas. Only fifteen percent of the planet is livable. The rest, you don't dare get caught in or you are sure to perish.

The best part about the planet the colonists find is deep in the Paladeus Mountains in the great canyons which they call the Paladeus Canyons. The canyons go one hundred miles straight down. It is thousands of miles long at the end. Most of the ships land right at the tip where one can walk across without having to cross the canyon. There is lava in the bottom in the middle where the equator is, but on the north and south, there is no lava in the bottom of it but a liquid-like substance one hundred miles down. If you have a space suit on, you can dive off the edge and free fall literally forever. Due to the gravity of the rocks, free falling, they can reach a terminal velocity of anywhere from one hundred miles/qs, which is per quarter sector to one hundred and thirty miles/qs.

If they didn't use jet packs, they would fall too fast, making a quarter sector fall last only a few moments. The jet packs on the suit kick on before they hit the bottom and fly them back up to the top. These conditions only happen for a few rests out of the heap, depending on where the canyon is on the orbit, but it is the most exciting and funnest part of the planet.

Later, after Corton experiments with some of the slime that Sparks was caught in, they find that if you fill your lungs with the slime, you can free fall with just rocket packs on your wrists and ankles. Right when you hit the bottom, you can dive into the water, and with a light belt, you can go real deep and see the fish-like plants that swim in the water. Most everything in the water is afraid of the divers, except for what they call the cretarius, which one of the colonists, Dr. Baldren, discovered while diving one day.

It is a vicious thing. There aren't many of them, but you can tell their territory because they eat everything in it. So, if there is nothing swimming there, you know not to go there. There are a few casualties during this process, but after the loss of three lives, Dr. Baldren is able to program a computer to analyze the safe havens in the water-like substance called woosh. It is a little thicker than water.

Not everyone does the free falling because it is for extreme adrenaline addicts, mostly those who are a little more high strung than the others. You can tell a difference. Everybody has good attitudes and motivations. There are never arguments or fights because of the high level of education everybody has. Everybody goes from one doctorate to the next. The more doctorates you have, the more seniority you have. It doesn't matter how much time it takes you to get them or how you have them, but usually the smarter ones, such as Corton and his brother, have the highest level of doctorates.

For a person that has an IQ of one hundred, it would take ten heaps to get a doctorate. For a person with an IQ of two hundred, it would take about five. But Corton himself has an IQ in most things of about a thousand. In some things, such as mathematical calculations, his IQ is off the charts. All of his brother's IQ levels are readable but very high. Before the brothers were old enough to even dress themselves, they were reading, writing, and programming things that most adults could not even do. They are phenomenal scientists, to say the least.

Now Corton is one to calculate every risk involved with everything, and free falling doesn't seem logical to him. But Ronson, on the other hand, even though he isn't high strung, is the type of person that has to try everything at least once just so he can calculate its variables and risks.

So, after free falling for almost a sector, he finally gets back to where Corton is, in their lab. He tells Corton, "You know, everybody ought to try that just once." He says it with a smirk on his face, knowing deep in his heart that he will never do that again.

"Yeah, why is that?" Corton asks.

"That way they will know for sure that they shouldn't do it again."

"Did you go all the way down to that liquid-like substance, the woosh?" Corton asks.

"Yes, but after falling down about halfway, my stomach was so queasy I had to kick in the jet packs and float a little while. That's why it took me so long to get back up here. Although there were a handful of people down there, I still felt somewhat out of place."

That's when Corton says, "Yeah, with good reason."

"Yeah, what's that?"

"We're all work and no play. And that's just play," Corton tells him.

"Well, you gotta live a little every now and then," Ronson says. "Besides, how would I calculate the risk for others if I don't experiment myself?"

Another thing about this planet is that there are no insects, but after the first heap, the first full orbit, there is a thing called floaters. Now floaters are about one inch in diameter. They don't fly, and they don't navigate. The scientists study them intricately and find absolutely not one use for them whatsoever. But if they land on you for more than a few seconds, it will turn into a whelp, and then the center of it will fester up into a boil. After a couple of moments, you are in agonizing pain all over your body.

There is no repellent and no way to control them. But as long as you are moving or if you are under a canopy, you do not have anything to worry about. The suits prevent the floaters from landing on people, all except for on their faces, necks, and hands, the most painful parts it seems. It is very rare that anybody gets floaters on them, but if you fall asleep during a sector of time and one lands on you, you will surely wake up in pain. There is no cure and no relief. The pain lasts for twenty moments, and it goes away just as quick as it comes up.

They call these the floaters of death. In short, they just call them floaters. The reason they call them the floaters of death is because as soon as they land on you, they absorb into your skin and die, as they do with anything they land on. So, if you see one inch circles anywhere on the planet, you know what they are. After fifty spots of time, they disappear with other plants. Extinction happens on this planet several times a heap, but where one thing becomes extinct, another thing evolves or adapts. It is never the same, except for the beast of the field which everybody fears, the viciaclaw.

During the short age of the floaters, a young girl named Zeleena is out on a platform built by her parents and some other people. After a while of studying, she lays her head back, looking up toward the sky. Little does she know, as she falls asleep, that only one eye is closed. Her eye being moist, a floater lands right on it. After a horrifying scream, her parents come running around. She is dancing all over the place. They cannot figure out what is wrong until twenty moments later when she says, "It was my eye. I can't see out of it now."

The black part of her pupil looks like it has layers from a dark purple at the tip to a light gray as it enters into the colored part of the eye. She says, "I can't see out of my eye." She keeps blinking it, so they take her to the lab and examine her eyes. She can't see anything out of that eye.

Now in the middle of the lab there is a glass dome in the ceiling that is a part of the roof, and through it, you can see the closest planet as the paradise belt planet comes around its orbit. After they run tests on Zeleena's eye, her pupil clears up, leaving it in the state that it was in before, but still she is unable to see until she looks up through the ceiling, up through the glass dome. She begins to stare through the glass dome.

All of the sudden, she realizes that she can see the craters on the far away planet. She blinks the eye that is damaged and she can't see it, but when she opens up the eye that is damaged, she can see it. That's when she tells the technician over the lab, " I can see the craters on that planet over there."

He looks at her and says, "No one can see the craters on that planet without a telescope. It's too far away."

She then replies, saying, "I see three craters and one crater in the middle of all of them, bigger, and I see another crater on the side of it. It kinda looks like a cone with some kind of berries in it."

Now the young technician has been studying the planet. It comes around three times a heap, and it is a very beautiful view. That's when he tells her, "Draw me a picture of the craters that you see."

She draws exactly what he has been studying. He says, "That's impossible! How can you see that far?"

She says, "I can see the smaller ones even better, and I also see the ice caps where it blasted the edges up higher when the crater was made."

That's when he becomes very interested in her eye and the damage the little floater has done. After observing her optical nerve through her pupil, he realizes that the boil has turned into a multi-layered lens, making her eye telescopic. If you are staring her in the face, you can hardly tell that her eye is damaged at all.

After she sees the planet and is able to see so far, she tells her dad that she is kinda glad that it happened. Her dad does not understand this and is kinda pricked to his heart.

She says, "Dad, this is the most beautiful thing I've ever seen. I can see the faraway planets as if they are in my hand." That's when she realizes if she stares out in space long enough, she can see galaxies far away. Zeleena has turned something tragic into something beautiful and wonderful, and now, she is able to see into space without a telescope.

Not long after this, the floaters all die out and go extinct. Some of the other kids make fun of Zeleena in a round about way until they find out that she can see far off even better than they can with a telescope. That's when they all go around trying to find floaters so they can have their eye do the same thing, but it is too late. The parents think to themselves that they are glad these are now extinct because it is a very painful thing. They realize the phenomenal thing that happened to Zeleena was just a one time thing. Now Zeleena is young, at the age of thirteen, but little does she know, her usefulness is going to play a great part in the future.

There is one animal called the githarat. A githarat is a terrible beast. It lives in the northern hemisphere and can take extreme heat and blistering cold. It can literally eat anything. Some say they have even seen it eat rocks.

The githarat is the horrible name they gave it because it will eat the metal off the ships if they are in its pathway. Although there are not many, you can tell its pathway because it eats everything in its path. Its size is humongous, coming in at the size of about two men and right at four hundred kilos. At around about eight hundred pounds, this thing clears a really good path and leaves a terrible mess behind it, especially through the swamps, if you need to be going that way. When the mess dries up, it turns into a really nice pathway. What it doesn't eat, it pushes out of the way with extreme force. It has elephant-like feet with claws on the back of them that point downward. Its thick leathery hide is around five inches thick, impenetrable.

There was a scientist that made a hammock out of the plant life and hung it between two trees, apparently in the pathway of a githarat. They only reason they know the githarat got him is because when they went to look for him, only the ends of the hammock were still tied to the trees. The rest was gone, and he was nowhere in sight. There was no trace of him. Apparently, he had been completely consumed.

Sightings of the githarat cease after about the fourth heap of being on the planet. Apparently, they traveled through the center of the equator. They might have made it through the blistering cold, but there is no way they could have made it through the lava on the hottest part of the equator. If you have a fire around the crops, the plant-like animals will not come and eat the crop because they can't take the heat.

The worst thing about the githarat was that one season, little flying creatures with a one inch needle-like mouth flew around them. When it poked the needle-like mouth into you, it filled up its tail with your blood and left a nasty sting that would paralyze you for a quarter sector almost instantly upon the bite. It would feed the blood to the little eggs that it laid on the githarat's hide just below the leathery surface. So, if you were near the githarat or in its path, you were sure to perish, and some did. But these little flying creatures only lasted one season. No more deaths were reported after that.

Before Dr. Glyria and Dr. Lavemen's lives were extinguished, they downloaded data that showed a solar system in a nearby galaxy. If they could establish another vessel, they could travel to an Earth-like planet that stays seventy-five degrees year round, a paradise above all planets with a solar life of billions of heaps. This data was placed into one of the escape shuttles, along with plants, animals, and everything they needed to re-establish life on another planet. Dr. Glyria, Dr. Laveman, the second commander, and the captain were about to get on this vessel when the departure switch was accidentally timed so they had to get on one of the smaller ships. When they did, they perished in the sun along with many other ships.

Although the space station burnt up and melted down, its melted metal entered into the atmosphere, part of it going into the belt and part of it going into the ice, what didn't burn up, but the other ship that would help them re-colonize a planet orbited in space. Nobody knew this because radio communication would not reach that far because of the hostile solar flaring of the sun, but the ship orbited on the dark side of the planet and remained intact. With this ship being unmanned, it was basically hovering in space, waiting on re-entry, settled into a stationary orbit.

Now the radio communication from the vessel that Glyria and Dr. Laveman prepared was programmed to re-establish communication with all the vessels. But it is thousands of miles away, until one spot when Corton is working on some radio communication and gets the radios to a frequency that can be heard for thousands of miles. He establishes a link-up between the rover ship that he is staying in and what is now going to be the mother ship. Corton is able to download the data from the mother ship. Now this mother ship, it can hold maybe a hundred people, but life support on it would only be for about six leans to a heap.

The scientists reason among themselves after finding out that they have a new mother ship how they can build a new space station that will be able to travel through a hostile space environment. Although it is not big enough to hold everyone, it will be by the time they get it built. They reason among themselves that it may take a hundred heaps. They pretty much come to the realization that they will be here until they die, but their children's children will be able to carry on if they get started on it now.

Ronson, after making navigation plans, establishing the work load, and establishing a time line of how long it will actually take, realizes that using the ships that remain, it will be possible to get a space station big enough to hold two thousand people, especially after finding out some of the resources on this planet are suitable for space metals. Some are even better than what they had before.

During Corton's experiments with the slime, he realizes why the ground sucked it up so fast. After taking a jar of it and setting it in the room, he finds it purifies the air and fills it with oxygen. These plant-like animals are the reason the air on the planet is so purified. After sitting in a jar for three rests with the lid off, there is no bacteria whatsoever in the ship's lab room.

This substance along with others from the planet are going to move people's longevity of life from a few heaps to hundreds of heaps. After discussing their many new developments with the other scientists, they realize that it may not even take twenty heaps to re-establish a full working station able to travel through space. It certainly will not take a hundred.

But even after their experiments, the life expectancy of a man is still one hundred and twenty heaps, but it is one hundred and twenty of the healthiest heaps that man has ever lived. They don't know why, other than an ancient saying, but after a hundred and twenty heaps or a little before, their bodies just exhaust. So, nobody really knows when they are going to die, only that they live to be over one hundred. Now that doesn't mean you can't get killed. To live a healthy life, you have to live a smart life, too. But sometimes, even the smartest get killed, tragically so, especially on the paradise belt planet, or PDP as they are now calling it.

Underground, during one lunch session, Que decides that they are going to have to get to work on how to provide enough food for three people for at least eight heaps without them going into cryogenics. He tells the others, "If two of us stay awake, we will have enough food on board for four heaps the way it is. If we cultivate plant life, three of us can live six to eight heaps."

In Que's heart, he has always thought of himself as an overseer that likes to get things done, but sometimes his pride gets in the way. Sometimes he says things he doesn't mean, but he always does the right thing with the crew. Even then, he is often taken the wrong way. So, his social skills are not up to par as some would say. Serena, seeing right through him, sees that he acts like a tough guy, but she realizes right from the start that he has a very tender heart. She is quickly won over.

After the first two leans of cultivating plant life, Que is tending to this one plant called Terano which produces a red, sweet, scrumptious fruit which is his favorite. Selena walks up to the door and watches him without him knowing she is there. The plant is slooped over. The top is now touching the soil. With a sobering voice, Que says, "Oh no, little buddy, please don't die."

He props the plant up and moves the soil around. The next spot of time when he goes in, she comes to the door and finds him weeping. She comes in and says, "Que, what is wrong?" She puts her hand on his shoulder.

He says, "No matter what I did, it didn't save it."

69

She looks at the plant and sees that it is dead as he says, "This was my favorite fruit."

"Oh you poor thing," she says. "You really are sensitive, aren't you?" As she says this, she pulls his head close to her chest and puts her other arm around his back.

When Que feels her warmth toward him, he puts his arms around her waist, securely pulls her up close, and looks up at her face. She looks down into his eyes and says, "You surprised me."

"What do you mean?" he asks.

"You're not what you pretend to be at all. Are you?"

"I don't understand. What do you mean?"

"Well, you're a wonderful person. That's all," she answers.

His heart melts. He falls in love, forgetting all the sarcasm, all the trouble, and all the pain he has suffered. He closes his eyes and hugs her even tighter.

Now Serena already loves Que, and after he hugs her like he does, she loves him even more. That's when she says, "We will grow another plant in its place, and we will work on it together."

Que says, "I would like that very much."

They get another seed, and after it becomes a sapling, they transplant it. After a few rests, it begins to grow fruit on it.

After several spots of time go by, Que's attitude has completely changed. That's when Fleece asks Serena, "What's going on with him? He is like a totally different person. I can hardly believe my eyes."

Serena smiles and says, "Maybe he's in love."

"Serena, I don't know what it is," Fleece tells her. "All I've got to say is keep up the good work because it's been right pleasant the past few rests, especially working with Que. He compliments me on everything, and he even gave me credit to you for some of the things that he was in charge of that he should have gotten credit for."

As Serena begins to walk out of the room, she turns around and says, "If I didn't know better, Fleece, I would think you are beginning to like Que a lot."

Fleece says, "Yeah, we're becoming good friends, I believe. He's really a nice guy after you get to know him."

Now the stress of being in the bottom of a sandpit that is miles beneath the surface is no different than being in space, thousands of miles from your destination, but finally the computer comes online and says, "We have reached the edge. It seems to be a cliff."

"Let's walk along its edge and see if there is a way out," Que says.

After walking for a couple of leans, the computer says, "We are going down levels instead of up." Serena puts in a trajectory to go upward and find the shortest path.

That's when Que says, "If we could just analyze this stuff...Computer, is there any way that we can get this soil inside to where we can analyze it?"

"Negative, not without contaminating the entire ship," the computer replies. "There is a probe that can be released out of one of the small bays, but once the bay is opened all the way, it will not be able to be closed. It will be filled with the soil that we are needing to analyze. The components in there will be damaged, but the probe will still be hooked to the ship once we open the compartment. We can do analyzation from there without contaminating the rest of the ship."

After the three get together and articulate on this, they realize this is the only way they are going to be able to find out what the stuff is, so the computer is instructed to open the door one eighth of an inch. When it does, nothing happens. None of the stuff goes into the compartment. They conclude that the material is larger than one eighth of an inch. Que instructs the computer to open the compartment another sixteenth of an inch. After doing so, a small amount of the debris enters into the compartment. That's when Que commands that the computer shut the door so it will not ruin the components on the inside of the compartment.

A small robotic arm on the probe as it sits on its landing bay extends out and takes a sample of the material. After analyzing it closely and running several tests, the probe comes back with a negative response. "The material is not on the periodic table. It does not match anything on record." The probe then puts a torch on it and registers it with a thermometer probe. It stays at a constant seventy degrees, no matter if it is heated or if it is frozen.

Que says, "We do not know if we are in the scorching sun or on the blistering freezing side of the planet. Even if we reach the surface, how are we going to know when to come up out of this pit?" The others do not have an answer.

Now Que loves Serena with all his heart. He waits on her hand and foot. She constantly has a smile on her face because of the things he does for her and some of the nicest things he says. He tells her every spot how much he loves her. The captain and commander were the only ones on board the space station that were able to give two people permission to marry and ordain two people to be husband and wife. There was a bishop or two on board, but they were in cryogenics. As far as Que and Serena are concerned, they are husband and wife already, but they want to make it right.

That's when they talk about being married and saying their vows before the captain. That's when Que says, "I've got no problem with Fleece being in charge." Serena agrees that she has no problem with it either.

They both say, "Well, that makes him captain of the ship.

Doesn't it?"

"Is there anybody here that objects?" Que asks.

"I don't hear anybody objecting," Serena answers. "Do you, Fleece?"

"Nah, I don't object. I will be the captain."

The computer comes on and says, "I will be the witness."

That's when they all laugh, and Fleece says, "Well, it's settled then. Let's perform the ceremony."

Now Fleece, being a dedicated scientist and committed to his work, is always crunching numbers and coming up with formulas. Being the scientist that he is and now captain of the ship, after marrying Que and Serena, he comes to the conclusion that this stuff they are in may have saved their lives.

A few leans after the ceremony, Serena conceives and is now going to have a baby. That's when the couple begins to articulate on whether or not to go into cryogenics since they do not want to have their baby underground, but they also do not know if they will ever make it to the surface either.

In the colony, a heap has gone by, and communication with about one hundred people has been lost. They can only assume the worst. Their ships have been taken over by others. At this rate, they will all be dead in ten heaps. Re-population has begun, but there are only about twenty children so far. Re-population is down to a minimum because there is so much to do to stay alive on this planet. You have to wear your space suit most of the time because the plant life is so poisonous in some areas. They have to keep the expecting mothers and the infants completely shielded from any type of toxins.

Every new terrain has to be tested because of the sink holes. They have pretty much discovered that if the plant life is gone, they have to go around that part of the land, which adds to their journey. Up north toward the north pole of the planet, after one heap of surveying, they realize that the planet does turn slightly, but it turns counter clockwise. It takes about a heap for it to move a mile. So, every hundred thousand heaps or so, it will have a full rotation, counter clockwise if you're looking at it from the sun's point of view.

A specially designed type of drone called cybernetic drones are built by one of the scientists to withstand the cold pressure, made mostly from the gel from some of these plants that doesn't freeze and doesn't burn up. The metals found here are not your average metals. Some of them do not melt no matter how hot they get, but mixed with some of the chemicals found on the planet, they will mold and solidify. The drones are very well put together with these metals. So, they are sent to take pictures of the rest of the planet.

The first area the drones go to is the cold part which is the darkest. The first drone sent there is not recovered, but by the footage that it sends back through the radio communication, it is horrifying. There are constant blizzards and constant storms that keep the ice on the mountains three or four miles thick in the short time that it stays in the cold. Apparently, all the water is evaporated from one side of the planet, the hot side, and the moisture accumulates to the cold side of the planet. By the time it gets to where it will precipitate into rain, it freezes. Then, the harsh storms carry it to the mountaintops.

Probes are sent to the peaks of the mountains. Most of them stop working when they hit the hot side on the equator if they don't burn completely up. Radio frequencies are established with the help of scientists which make it possible for the probes to send back messages from this harsh environment.

Because of the resources, a super probe is created which later on is able to go anywhere on the planet. It is an android type probe with arms and legs. It can walk upright or on all fours. It can climb. It can fly. It can swim. It can go through the freezing cold of the lakes. The only thing it is not able do is go through the lava, only because it solidifies in the lava and once the lava hardens coming out of the heat of the sun and turns into rock, the probe is stuck in there. Some have been able to radio communicate after going through the lava, but they are not able to get out of the rock after the lava hardens.

When certain plant life grows on this planet, they make some of the purest air that you can breathe. The air has to be constantly monitored. Some plants put out poisonous gasses, some poisonous acids. All plants are alive. They do not have a brain, but they can eat just like an animal. The animals that do have brains adapt and can move very fast.

One animal in particular, the beast of the field, is about twenty feet long and is called a viciaclaw. It deserves its name because of its vicious claws. It has eight legs with three inch sharp claws on each paw. Each paw has about ten of these laser sharp claws. One claw can snatch a man up.

They can't catch one of these things at first but imagine that it weighs about twelve to fourteen hundred pounds. It can run upright on the back four legs with the front four and the front half of its body sticking straight up in the air. Or it can run on six legs with two straight up, or it can run with all eight legs. Each leg is like an arm. It is able to grab and do things with all the legs just like it can with the front two.

The viciaclaw's mouth has a row of teeth in the front. The first is like a canine. The span of its mouth is about one foot wide. Once it opens its mouth, it has a row of sharp teeth going all the way throughout the roof of its mouth to the back of its throat, and they all point to the back, each one a little less sharp as it goes back. It does that on the sides of the tongue on the jawbone. The tongue is like rough tainted hide.

They didn't find this out until one of them was snatched up by a viciaclaw by his midsection with one of the claws and carried one hundred miles. When they found him, his leg had been bitten off and part of his midsection. These animals don't kill for sport. They only kill for survival. About a half a mile away from the body, they found the viciaclaw. It died from not being able to digest the bones that it ate. It was not able to pass them through. They know it died an agonizing death because when the search party came upon it, it was still alive but in agony.

They spent three spots observing it, but it was too large to bring back to the camp. So, after they studied it a while, they cut its head off and brought it back for the scientists to do more research on it. They also brought back the claws to be studied. After this, the fear of the viciaclaw began dying out, being how they knew if it ate one of them, it would spit them out a quarter sector later and die. Several people have been extinguished by the viciaclaw, but because it was trying to eat people, it almost went extinct, too.

Radio communication with the few ships in the south every now and then establishes the fact that they are catching and making pets out of the youth of these viciaclaws. It seems they have a unique usefulness without taking their life. The females give out a milk-like substance that turns into an adhesive that will hold steel or any other type of metallic material together. It is better than a weld. That is when they begin to breed them for the females so they don't have to generate electricity for welds for the space station. Out of a quart of the viciaclaw's milk, they can make about twenty-five gallons of these special adhesives.

Another special usefulness for the milk-like substance is for the congelling of glass to metal to keep it from leaking out atmosphere. Along with that and hundreds of other uses for parts of the viciaclaw, they discover that their dark black claws seem to be some kind of hard crystal. It is one of the hardest substances known on the planet. They later use this in machinery to cut some of the metals which are going to be used to make the space station, which cuts the build time immensely.

The shuttle ships are still able to fly out into space because the gravity on the dark side for some reason is lighter, and it doesn't take as much fuel. After about a heap, they are able to find enough fuels to get the rockets on some of the ships to full potential. The only way to blast out of gravity is to have some kind of fuel. Although there are three other types of energy, there isn't the type that will help lift the shuttles off the planet.

So, after a heap and a half, the scientists get together a team, and a couple of the space ships go to outer space. They are trying to figure out a way to dock to the bigger ship that is left out there. It is in perfect condition, but there is no way to dock to it. So, they have to leave one ship in space suits, tie ropes onto each man, and go over to the other ship to open it up. After two or three times, they finally build a hatch. They leave a crew of twenty men there that constantly work on the station, and every couple of leans, they trade out as they are needed on the planet.

They now have ten people which are now world leaders. They are very sophisticated and very knowledgeable in the planning of the voyage to the new galaxy. The creation of a new station is now well on its way. A new hope.

After warp drive, Commander Alexander is exhausted from the stressful detoxing and de-cryogenics. He is tired and alone, not knowing where he is or what to do. After warping into the outer edges of the galaxy, he now has to figure out a way to get back. Only this time, the warp drive energy sources are completely used up. Without a warp drive, he cannot get there fast enough to figure out what happened to everyone else. After he gets the ship turned around to head back to the solar system he has just come from, he plots a course and navigates with conventional engine sources. After he gets up to speed, rocket fuel is exhausted.

After a sector of sleep, if that's what you want to call it... terrible nightmares of being alone and being without oxygen and food... the commander wakes up with a horrible sweat. He then walks over to the showers, and after showering off, he wraps a towel around his waist and begins to look for food. Now, there are several varieties of food on board, and if one planned it right, they could live indefinitely on the shuttle, some say. It has seeds, dirt, and other means of growing and producing food. It also has a small aquarium which produces a large number of varieties of seafood: fish, small shrimp, and others.

After several spots of time, the commander looks through the seeds and comes across a seed he has never seen before. The bag has been handled so much that it has worn off the first part of it. The last part of it is "-ffee", which he calls effy. It has a horrible smell. It is green and about half the size of a pinky nail, and it does not grow very well. After cultivating this seed for a long period of time and watching saplings die one after another, he realizes this is not a primary source of food.

Then one spot, while in the lounge quarters, some of the seeds fall into the plate of the dehydrating process for the food he is about to eat. When the commander sticks it in the hydrator, the seeds heat up, turn black, and the outside shell pops off. When he pulls out the tray, he sees what he has done and rakes them off into a drinking flask that is nearby.

In the hydrating process, the commander will heat up a flask of water, put the seeds in a long tray, and then there will be a pour line in the back of the tray where he will pour the hot water. The seeds will absorb the water and begin to grow, then he will plant them in a special type of soil.

This time, not realizing that he has grabbed the flask that he stuck the black burnt seeds in, he puts it in the microwave. After microwaved particles heat up the water, it also heats up the seed and turns it black. Now, not knowing that the water is black, the commander begins to pour it into the tray. The process is very slow, and as he does it, he sees that the water is black. He had realized before he started pouring the water that it had a strong aroma, a smell he had never smelled before.

The commander pours the substance into a flask that he can see through and realizes he had left the beans in there. Now water is a precious resource on this vessel. Every drop of water is regained out of the air, out of the clothing, and every precious drop of fluid out of the body is reprocessed. If anything gets wasted, it could mean your life. Knowing that precious resources cannot be wasted, he decides to analyze the fluid from the beans, and after it tests to be safe, he strains it and drinks the fluid out of it anyway. When he does, he thinks it is the most horrible bitter taste he has ever tasted.

Shortly after this, the commander begins to feel funny. After about ten moments of dancing around while he is cultivating the seedlings that he is growing, he realizes how different he feels. "Wow! I feel really good!" he thinks to himself.

Commander Alexander tells the computer to play some classic music, something that is upbeat. The next thing he knows, he finds himself singing and yelling on board. He thinks to himself, "Wow! What a way to wake up!"

He says, "Computer, run further analysis on these black

beans."

After a short moment of analyzation, the computer comes back and says, "This is an ancient seed from the planet Earth. Every ship was equipped with one pound of seeds so it could be cultivated on the new planet."

"How is it used, Computer?" he asks.

"The seeds are taken and dried out to approximately five percent hydration. After this process, they are then taken and cooked until they pop very loud and the shell comes off, until they are a medium to dark brown shade of color. Then, they are ground up and put into boiling water. After it is strained, it is drank. Its original name was coffee."

So, Commander Alexander spends a little time burning all of the beans except for five of them. After grinding the coffee up, he uses it very, very conservatively. After several leans go by, the coffee is exhausted. After many conversations and articulating with the computer about the coffee, he has learned the different ways of putting sweetener in it and other ways of preparing it, even sprinkling the dried out, already used coffee grounds on other foods and eating them. He has gotten the same results, but now it is all gone.

After conversing with the computer once more, he asks the computer why he cannot get the saplings to grow. The computer tells him that there has to be a certain elevation of gravity for the plant to produce well, usually very high up with less oxygen than other plants. The computer also says, "Commander, I should have warned you. This substance is known to be highly addictive."

"No kidding," the commander replies.

After the first three heaps, several things on board have been exhausted. Coffee seems to be the most precious out of all of it. A large seed called avocado is another ancient seed that becomes a precious resource. After eating one, his energy level soars with ease. He is able to cultivate a four feet tall tree that yields four avocados every three leans.

The garden room is about twelve feet high. It has grating ceilings and grating floor with special lights shining through them. Around its walls, it has two sets of shelves, four feet off the ground and eight feet off the ground. They also have the special lights in the grating shining upward and downward. Everything that is processed is re-entered into the soil. Beneath each planter, there is a small hole for drainage. All fluids go into the hole and down a special tube, and then they are reprocessed, along with the other fluids on the ship. Nothing is wasted.

There is a robot android that keeps up the cultivation of the plants, but after four heaps, it completely wears out. All the parts for it on board are used up. The commander starts building a synthetic type android, but with the lack of materials on board and the lack of know how, he comes to a complete stop. After running out of resources to rebuild his only friend, he realizes for the first time how alone he really is. That's when it hits him. "God, I don't think I can do this alone," the commander says.

Chapter 6
Time Line

A new time line is established. If they don't lose anybody else and everybody is able to work on the space station throughout the heap, they can have enough built in ten heaps to take off. After Corton studies the slime even more, they figure out that you can sleep indefinitely in this gel. So, they decide the passengers that wish to sleep will be put in the gel for long term cryogenics, and those needed to navigate the ship will be put in regular cryogenics to be woken up for their shifts.

The slime is now called space gel. It has a million and one uses. If you get a cut on you and apply some of the gel, it heals the cut within moments. It completely cauterizes and sterilizes any wound. The wound closes instantly. If you put it on your eyes, you can see in total darkness. They even find out that you can get closer to the sun when the gel is on your skin but only for a little while and not in direct sunlight. If you see the sun, you are dead. After a while, the heat gets to be too much, and you have to journey around to the cooler part of the planet.

On the space station, progress of work has tripled. There are now three hundred people living on the space station two heaps into the work of it. This once was a small ship, able to hold about a hundred people. Now, it is able to hold several hundred people. New ships have been created to fly from the hostile planet's surface to this new space station. New space suits have also been created.

They find out that once your lungs are filled up with the space gel, there is no need for oxygen, so the workers are able to work without a time line. Sparks and Julia spend a lot of time investigating and cultivating new foods. Some of the nutrition of the plant life on the planet is so intense that you cannot eat more than once every few spots. The food is so rich that too much consumption would make you obese in a matter of spots. Because people are so used to eating, they make flavored gum out of the sap of some of the plants that doesn't dissolve in your mouth.

Fluids are a must. This is the only problem in the space suit. Fluids have to constantly move through your body, so the scientists come up with a solution in which all the waste is recycled and reintroduced with a little bit of the proteins from the plant life, making everybody stronger and more adequate to work.

Some people are transforming. The families able to reproduce are no longer held back on reproduction as they were before. The second heap, eighty-nine children are introduced, mostly from the young married couples. Twins are born, some triplets. At this rate, repopulating the new space station will be no problem. In the first two heaps, around two hundred people perish. But half of those are repopulated, so there are still around one thousand people living on this planet.

They are all closely knitted. Those that were in the southern hemisphere have now moved to the northern hemisphere along with all of their machinery. Houses are built to where they can withstand the residual heat and cold. Eventually all they have to do is move from house to house. They don't have to rebuild the houses because they do not burn up.

They find more and more dangers on the planet's surface. There is a dangerous reptilian which is about one hundred and fifty feet long. They do not know this at first, but near the north pole of the planet, it lives underground, mostly where the sinking sand is which is actually not sand at all but a substance they now call Sanulite. This reptilian can swallow a man whole. It is about as big around as a tree trunk. It moves very fast and has laser sharp teeth.

The neighbor of one of the scientists wakes up very late one spot to a horrifying scream. It doesn't get dark on this planet, but it is late in the spot. When he goes outside, he sees that the reptilian has wrapped itself around the scientist's house four or five times. The scientist is halfway in its mouth from his feet down, and the reptilian is swinging him backward and forward trying to swallow him. When he woke up, he was half eaten. Apparently, he was attacked while he was sleeping. He is beating the reptilian on the head with all he has. Every time he does, he goes a little farther into the mouth.

One of the other scientists grabs a laser cutter, goes about ten feet down from where the snake-like creature is, and starts trying to slice its head off about ten feet down from its mouth, assuring that it will not cut the scientist being eaten in half. When it makes the first whack, it only cuts about halfway through. That is when the reptilian comes untangled from the house and begins to squirm. The laser should have cut all the way through, but apparently the hide on this thing is a lot tougher than they think. When it comes untangled from the house, it hits the scientist that has the laser cutter, knocking him about ten feet back and breaking his arm and leg.

When the reptilian creature swings over, it swings by the top of him, missing him the first time. When it swings back around, he holds the laser up, and that's when it cuts the reptile in half a little farther down from the first cut. Only this time, the laser was closer and able to cut deeper. That's when the rest of those watching gather together and hold its mouth open. It takes about ten people to pry it open. When they get the scientist that was being eaten out, one of his legs is broken in about three different places from where it chopped down trying to swallow him, and a couple of his ribs are fractured.

Broken bones, because of the nutrition, will heal in a spot of time. All broken bones are healed including fractures to the skull. The healing rate is phenomenal unless the injuries are too severe like those from the eight-legged viciaclaw whose head and claws are still in the lab being observed. After a while, the teeth they pried from the jawbone of the viciaclaw dry and crystallize. It is like a diamond without any blemish, laser sharp. Placed on the end of a piece of steel, it can drill through anything which cuts time even further on building the space station.

The construction of the space station is the most unique of all. Panels are made from the hide of the reptilians. When solidified, they can withstand the actual penetration of the radiation of the sun. So, the space station is layered with these one hundred feet reptilian hides which are harder than steel. Most of these are later on replaced, but for now, they are light, strong, and can resist almost anything especially harsh climate changes.

With this new gel, new found minerals and metals, and plant and life forms, they think they can sustain life indefinitely for those that want to make it to the new planet. But they will take a chance on sleeping the whole time there at the risk of not even making it at all. How they have made it this far, they just don't know. They should have all died in the Planeterial.

One spot on the planet, a young couple is picnicking under a tree. Now this is a peculiar kind of tree. It doesn't have leaves, but it has a lot of bark. While snacking on some of the grub, Sadey says to his fiance, Trina Husby, "Ow! Something hit me on the head, and I'm bleeding."

She looks down behind him as he lays his head down and passes out. There is a piece of bark about six inches long, about one inch thick, and about two inches wide at the widest part. It is jagged. She starts to pick it up, and when she does, eight legs fold out from the sides.

It bends halfway in the middle and halfway in the middle the other way, down the center. It gets up on all eight legs after she drops it. Then, it stands up on the folded half and looks at her. Two antennas fold out about two inches long and about the size of a stylus with what looks like eyes on the end of them. It walks over to the tree, goes back up to the part it fell from, folds its legs back in, pulls what seems to be eyes back in, folds itself back up against the tree where it came from, and disappears into the bark.

When she sees this, she is stunned for a moment, thinking that she might be seeing things. By this time, her fiance is almost awake. She says, "Are you okay?"

He says, "Yeah, I'm feeling fine now." He feels his head. The abrasion is gone, and the blood is dried up. He stands to his feet, and says, "What happened?"

"Well, you probably won't believe me if I tell you," she answers. "A piece of bark hit you in the head, then it turned into some type of arachnid, climbed back on the tree, and turned back into a piece of bark."

He says, "Okay, now, what really happened?"

"No, really that happened," she insists. "That tree right there that we've been sitting under."

He goes over to touch the tree, and every piece of bark on the tree tumbles to the ground. The pieces of bark fold in half and grow eight legs. Then, every piece of bark walks off about a thousand yards and disappears into the thicket of trees while erecting themselves back into the form a tree.

After Sadey sees this, he says, "I thought I had seen it all on this planet, but now, I think we are just scratching the surface."

She says, "Yeah, it makes sense. How else would a two hundred fifty heap old tree be able to survive? It would have to get up and move along with everything else. We just haven't been able to see it before. We better tell this to some of the leaders."

Now Sparks is on the radio when the young gentleman tries to relay the message about the bark. The scientists must have been busy and didn't pick up on the radio, so Sparks replies, asking what they said about the bark.

"These trees are not trees," they tell him. "They look to be so, but they're not. They're just exterior bark, but the bark is alive. We watched a piece fall off, hit me in the head, then fold up eight legs, and get back in the tree where it came from. When we went to touch it, every piece fell to the ground, walked away about a thousand yards, and then erected back up into what seemed to be a tree."

"Did anybody get hurt?" Sparks asks.

"I got a little gash in my head where it fell out of the tree onto my head, but I'm alright."

"You better get it checked into," Sparks says, "so you don't get infection. I'll relay the message to some of the scientists."

Now one spot soon after that, Sparks is out in the garden, and he notices that the vegetation is extremely large. The spot before, it was medium sized, but this spot, it is five times bigger. He quickly gets on the radio and gets a hold of Ronson and Corton to tell them about it. Ronson comes to the conclusion that this may not be a good thing.

Sparks tells him, "Yes, but this fruit is delicious. It is really,

really good."

Ronson says, "We are going to come and investigate."

They use a smaller ship to rover over to where Sparks lives, to where his shuttle is parked. As soon as they get out of the ship, that's when it happens. A terrible tremor! The whole planet shakes violently, and the ground opens up. It is terribly long. It opens up a fault line all along the border, taking another fifteen ships and killing almost one hundred people. It is horrifying! The ground will not stop falling out from beneath them.

It gets up almost to where the garden is, where Sparks and Ronson were once standing. They are now lying on the ground, fearing for their lives. Sparks gets up on his hands and knees and makes it to firm ground. When he does, he looks over the edge. It is molten lava as far as the eye can see. There is no getting across this. The rovers are not going to make it. It goes all the way over to the other side from the North pole all the way mid-way down to the South pole right through the paradise belt thousands of miles long, blocking the way for the travelers to get through.

In two rests, if they don't move, they will be in the blistering sun. Two rests to travel. If they aren't moving by then, they will perish. They gather up everything they can. There are several injured, a couple of them paralyzed completely. It is terrible. They spend three spots doctoring on those that are injured.

Ronson and his brother realize had Sparks not called them, they would not be alive. Now Sparks is extremely smart, but he likes the company of Ronson and his brother. So, every now and then when he finds something interesting, it gives him a good excuse to fellowship with them. This time, it paid off. Where their ship once was, there is now nothing but a fault line of lava, hundreds of miles long, resting where they would have been. They would have surely perished.

Their dad, who was working in the lab at the time of the quake did perish along with their mom who was standing outside. Fifteen ships plus their dad's perish in the fault line, several very valuable scientists. One is a navigation scientist very important to the work on the new station. He, along with all his work, is now gone. They think this is going to set them back at least a heap or two.

The only way to get across the open fault line is to fly across, and this takes rocket fuel. Ronson quickly figures out that the ships that were left by the hundred people that died will have to re-manned. Some of the ships are not going to make it because they do not have enough fuel. Fuel is a precious resource that they try not to use if they can avoid it. They quickly gather all the supplies they can and everything they can carry from the ships. They cover them with the stuff they built houses out of and hope they will be there when they come back around. They blast off and fly to the other side of the crater.

The fourth heap on the planet, many lives are lost due to the ground opening up hundreds of miles three times in a row. The third time, it takes out a bunch of people. Most of the ships are able to fly off before they sink down into the planet thanks to their scientists' fast thinking. They put a gravitational field on each ship, and any time the ground falls out from under the gravitational field, the rockets will fire off whether there is anybody in the ships or not. Instead of ships and lives being lost, at least this way the ships are saved.

This is a fail safe. The ships will be part of the space station, directly hooked to the space station as living quarters, which makes perfect sense. Just in case the space station goes out again, the ships will automatically eject instead of creating so much chaos like there was on the Planeterial. It took two spots to get them out last time, and they may not have two spots this time.

One spot, Ronson tells Sparks that he has to go to the space station, that it is his turn to work there, and asks him if he and his wife would like to go and do some lab work there. Sparks and his wife are really excited. They haven't yet been able to see the new space station, so they all get on Sparks' ship. After they are all strapped in and have their space suits on, they blast off. After leaving the gravitation of the planet's atmosphere, they enter into space. At first, it is like a little dot, as if it is nothing in space.

Julia sees the space station from afar off and says, "Wow! It really is small. Are we all going to be able to live on that?"

Ronson smiles. Corton chuckles at the idea of it and says, "We are still quite a ways a way. It will be a while before you actually see the space station."

They hit the impulse rockets and blast toward the space station a little faster. Now, with new developments, a nuclear propulsion system will pull the ships through space without rocket fuel, and solar power helps too. They just need the rocket fuel to take off. After about a quarter of a sector, the space station is big enough to see.

"Wow!" is all they can think. It is great! It is about a mile long, and it isn't even half built. The center is a stylus-like tube, and there are three wheels, one in the middle and one in between that and the end, and one on the other side as well. At the very end of the space station is where the rockets are and the rocket fuel. The design of it is that if one the nine engines blow, it still won't hurt the other engines or the ship and its crew, and it certainly won't destroy the whole station.

After another thirty moments of traveling, they finally reach the hull of the space station. The ship enters into a lock-in, then they are able to open the hatch and enter into the bay as the air pressure levels out. Each corridor has an air pressure lock. While one door is open, the other door has to be closed. This ensures life support for each corridor. If there is an explosion anywhere on the space station, it will be contained within a thirty feet radius of these corridors.

So far, one hundred and twenty ships have been docked and set up on the space station. Now, it is time to give the space station a name. That's when Sparks' wife, Julia, says, "It looks kinda like a bunch of flowers."

Sparks replies, "Yeah, it's quite a limonium."

When Ronson hears that, he quickly says, "Well, that would make a great name."

Sparks says, "The Limonium, a group of one hundred and twenty that makes a family of flowers."

Corton looks surprised and asks, "How did you know about that?"

He says, "I know a lot of things. You know I've got a really high IQ. I know I'm on the low end of the genius levels, but I still know a few things."

Corton just smiles and says, "Yeah, that will make a great name, the Limonium."

Now after five heaps, the space station is getting quite large. Ronson tells his brother, Corton, "With all these new metals and all these new inventions everybody's coming up with, I figure we will be well on the way in another three heaps or so even with the setbacks, but don't tell anybody. Just let them think it is going to be ten heaps like we planned. That way, if anything goes wrong and we get set back, there won't be any hardships, and if the plans go faster, then everybody will be that much more excited."

The cool thing about the new space station on the outside of it is the laser cannons that go around the whole ship that will cut three miles deep, anything in their pathway. There are several different colors of lasers. The first invention of lasers was red, then it went to blue, then green, then yellow. But this laser is pure white, almost atomic. It cuts anything in its path exactly as deep as it goes and no deeper. You can cut a layer of skin off without ever touching the next layer. It is thin enough to go between the skin layers. Thanks to this planet and the scorching sun that penetrates it, certain crystals are found that create this white laser light.

Two or three lives were invested in the creation of this laser. It was actually quite an accident. Two of the lab scientists were blasting infrared and the yellow laser together into this crystal when one little bitty dot of pin light went through the crack of a part of the crystal. When the scientist walked in front of it, it severed him in half. When the other scientist saw this, he went over and saw all the damage the laser had done but had not yet seen the laser light. When he bent over, it went right through his head. He pulled back, but it was too late. It had already cut into part of his brain.

After this, one other scientist in further development of the laser found a metal that it did not cut through on the face of the planet. Now this metal, Zafirm, is a soft metal and pliable, if you hit it softly. The harder you hit it, the harder it is. So, when this laser hit it, it ricocheted off because it was like hitting it with the force of an atomic explosion. When it ricocheted, it put a pin hole through the scientist's heart. Now normally, this would not kill anybody, but when the laser was going through, he moved a little bit, causing a little slice, hitting the thymus gland and causing him to go into cardiac arrest.

Due to the sensorization on his suit being damaged also by the small blast through him, the computer was unaware of his condition. He fell to the floor behind a counter as if he had bent down to do something. So, when the other technicians looked over, they didn't realize he was in trouble. His eyes were wide open as he thought to himself, "Help! I'm dying." Then, he took one deep breath as his eyes waxed over.

After that, safety measures were doubled up, but the laser has a million uses on board which help cut hard metals and develop this space station to be twice the size of the original space station with twice the power, twice the speed.

Now Tamia is a scientist that Sparks has not heard of or met yet. She was in the lower regions of the planet, along with hundreds of others, but is now working on the space station. Sparks and Julia have the pleasure of meeting Tamia. He likes her a lot, maybe even too much. For a moment, it seems that way to Julia, but then she quickly shakes it off and realizes that Sparks isn't that way. And neither is Tamia, she realizes after getting to know her. She is a wonderful person, well kept. Not high maintenance but well groomed, so to speak. She is very friendly at all times with a lot of knowledge without being a know it all. She has a lot to say, but she makes sure that you say a lot, too. That's what Julia likes about her.

Tamia works in one of the labs called the Sobering Lab. This is where all the sensors are made and designed by her. The greatest sensor she designs is one to detect any fault in any instrumentation on the whole ship. She also designs a special computer that will hold all the data, overlay it, check it in centrifugal dimensional form, and relay it back in layman terms with self diagnostics and self repair. Tamia is one of the smartest women on the planet with one of the highest IQs in over two thousand heaps.

She excavates down into the fault line with ropes and finds a large canyon that is opened up in a wall. It can't be seen from the surface if you are looking down, but if you are looking from the other side, you can see there is a great big opening. Upon the entry of the canyon, there is a certain glow about certain formations on the wall.

She begins to experiment with probes. First, she takes a temperature rating. It is a five thousand degree rock, and after she holds the probe on there for five or ten moments, she notices that the rock's core does not cool off. One of the greatest finds of all time, a five thousand degree heat source that doesn't burn out locked in a metal that doesn't melt.

She has an idea. She takes some of the high powered lasers that were invented for the space station, cuts a two feet circle around the rock, and then cuts a two feet line on the outside of the circle at an angle where it will fall off. Then she cuts the rock out, along with its precious metal. The good thing about this metal is that it does not get hot. You can touch it almost up to a point, but with five thousand degrees heat, you can't get very close to it on the side where the stone is exposed. The wonderful thing about the new found precious metal and the rock with the heat source is that it only weighs about three pounds, even in a three feet diameter.

She takes the already cut out piece and puts it in a cover, so when the cover is put over the rock source with the metal on the top and the bottom, it kills the heat source completely until you take the top off. Up to the surface, it goes. Upon arriving on the face of the surface, one of her team grabs the instrumentation and picks the whole unit up. When he goes to set it down, it rolls on its side, opens up, and the heat source goes by his leg. At five thousand degrees heat, it lights his pants on fire and gives him third degree burns all the way up his leg. He goes to screaming.

Now everybody is smart and knows what to do when there are burns. There is a plant that grows everywhere that looks like white milk if you break it open. If you squeeze on it while you break it, it will spray like a squeeze bottle. One of the women quickly grabs a handful of these and squeezes them out as she bends them in half. They break open and spray all over his leg. He is jumping up and down and screaming uncontrollably until he gets relief from this plant. As soon as she sprays this on his leg, it quits burning and creates a layer that keeps any infection from coming in.

Tamia also designs cameras that are able to take pictures millions of light centuries away which are some of her greatest work. She is well recognized for this development that she is able to make thanks to the new found crystals found on the planet's surface, thanks to the laser that was developed that is actually able to cut these crystals, and thanks to a few other things that were found on the planet.

Scientists come to the agreement that if this one planet gave them this much technology and cut their hundred heap building of this space station so much, what will other planets have to offer, and what resources will they have? So, cameras attached, Tamia begins to search through each galaxy for planets that are inhabitable, especially along the path to the planet that is inhabitable which some claim to be a paradise.

Most articulate that it will just be nice just to have a planet where you do not have to run from the sun or move constantly heap round. Others admit the same thing. Moving is hard. It is crucial to the development of some things to be stationary. Once on the space station, a lot of things were invented that couldn't be invented in three or four leans because of the constant moving.

One of Tamia's greatest inventions is the main camera on the space station, but even though she has a lens that can see thousands of light heaps away, when you look at a planet with it, you cannot see its surface. While she is down in the canyon a half a mile down from the surface, she finds a purple plant, a plant so rare that

95

nobody has ever seen one before. Tamia quickly takes the plant and the liquid substance she was looking at through a microscope, and she notices that its magnification lets her see an atom of the glass that is on the other side of the liquid.

After she looks at the plant's molecular cell structure, she quickly realizes that it is similar to Sanulite, except there is a particular movement. While she looks it, she sees that that they keep bonding with one another and reproducing. She thinks it particularly necessary to go ten thousand times greater, and that is when she sees it.

On the surface of the sample, it is actually healing itself after being exposed to atmosphere, turning into a crystallized substance, and then the next layer beneath it does the same, amplifying the next layer. That's when she gets the idea to apply it behind a lens to their main computer telescope.

After several rests, she develops another lens to put in the big telescopic camera which actually allows them to see microscopically at telescopic distances, one of the greatest inventions of all time. Now, she can see millions of light centuries away, look at a planet, and actually see the detail of its surface. It is amazing!

The camera takes millions of pictures of millions of different planets. That's when they discover that the planet they are planning to go to, the one the Planeterial passed up because of the malfunctions in navigation, has a surface too soft to live on. Although it has trees, bushes, and all kinds of plant life and animal life on it, anything heavier than three pounds will sink through the surface. The trees spread out wide and weigh less than two pounds. Once they grow above three pounds, they sink down into the surface of the planet.

All the readings came back perfect: oxygen levels, temperature, moisture. Every reading was perfect. But now, they know they were wasting their time planning to go there. It is uninhabitable.

Thanks to Tamia's invention, they are able to watch other planets. They find another planet in a galaxy called Rastour. It spirals in a circle like the Milky Way, and out of its center, another galaxy spirals. The galaxies are colliding. In between the two centers, on a far edge of the galaxy, there is a planet Tamia names Tyronius. The planet Tyronius has three small planets circling it.

In its solar system, the planet Tyronius rotates around the sun, and the planet Tib rotates around it. Now if you are looking at the planet Tyronius from the sun, you can see Tib rotate around the planet counter clockwise. It rotates a perfect spot. It has beautiful blue water. The continents go around the planet like pathways, like bridges across water, and each pathway is a different color. It has a north pole and a south pole, and it has a moon just like Earth's moon. On its moon, it has another small moon going around that moon. It is the most phenomenal thing. There are three of these planets like Tib that rotate around the planet Tyronius. just opposite of each other. One is half the size of the planet.

The solar system itself has twelve planets, each one more beautiful than the next. The fifth planet out has a set of rings that go twice the size of the planet out. Above that, it has another set of rings that go the size of the planet out. Above that, it has another white ring which is ice. This three ring planet is named after its rings, Threering planet. It glows a beautiful yellow but has a blue ring in the center, and in between the blue and the white ring, there is a lighter blue. It is absolutely astonishing!

Every thousand heaps, Tib will switch its rotation around the axis of Tyronius, and for the span of ten heaps, it will rotate into the shadows of Tyronius, leaving the planet's surface on its warmest side about three degrees below zero. But it only happens ten heaps every thousand heaps. In direct sunlight, heap round on the planet's surface, it is complete utopia, a fair weather between seventy-five and eighty-five degrees all heap round, except for when it storms. Then it will drop about five degrees. From what they study, it only rains at night time.

Now this solar system, being in the opposite direction of the other solar system that they found previously would have taken the same amount of time on the deceased star ship, the Planeterial, which burnt up in this solar system, would have taken to reach their previous destination. They are now more than two hundred heaps past their destination. If their star ship would not have crashed into this solar system, some would have perished on the new found planet. But thanks to the resources on this planet, they were able to find the galaxy Rastour which would have never been found, but their previous star ship would have never reached it from where they are now. But with the new star ship, it is a lot closer because of their advanced warp capabilities.

Underground, it has been six long heaps, and the computer estimates that they have elevated three miles. They only have two miles to go. Now, at the end of six long heaps and after being alone for a long time now, Fleece Charidon decides to wake up one of the other scientists. He knew from the start, and so did everyone else, that the two had realized there was not enough food on board and so had taken the opportune time to go into cryogenics. But now that Que and Serena are in hibernation and they have cultivated so many plants, there are plenty of resources for another person to be awake for several heaps.

But he can't decide which one will be more valuable to wake up at this time. After going over and analyzing each one's chart, he decides that Teah will be the best one suited for the job because she also has cultivation skills, and if need be, he can wake up the other scientist, also. Teah is de-cryogenilized. After waking her, Fleece brings her up to specs on all that has happened.

Progress is made coming up out of the hole, and a few leans later, the computer re-estimates that they may only have a few leans before reaching the surface, if they do not run into another cliff side. Suddenly, the alert buzzers go off and the computer comes over the intercom and says, "One of the robotic arms is damaged. Apparently, we have run into a cliff wall on the other side and now only have three robotic arms left.

"Well, that's not good," Teah says.

After a few moments of dealing with the horrifying news, Fleece says, "Quick, Computer, how far apart from the ship is the other ledge?"

"Approximately three feet from each side."

"Can the one robotic arm on the opposing side maintain the weight of the ship?"

The computer comes back and says, "It is more than capable."

"Then why can't we climb in between the two cliffs?"

The computer comes back and says, "Excellent idea, but I have already analyzed the situation and already navigated the climb. It is now in progress as we speak."

That's when Teah says excitedly, "Then that's going to make us reach the surface even faster."

Now, Teah, even though she is only fourteen, is very witty and quick on the draw. Before somebody can say a full sentence, she already has the answer and almost knows what to say to the next sentence or question. She can analyze somebody by their expression and just about articulate the whole subject without the other person saying more than a couple of words. Normally, she leaves a lot of people astonished. Being on a high genius level, like her colleague, Fleece, who is not much older than she is, they crunch numbers continually in their heads. Although they are continual companions, there is no romance between them at all which makes them even better friends.

After Teah woke up, they started a chess game, and because they are both so smart, the game has been going on for almost a heap now. Teah comes into the lounge quarters and says, "By the way, it's your move."

The game is just about at a halt as Fleece analyzes the computer board and realizes there are no moves to be made. Everything is completely blocked. He analyzes the killing components and realizes that whoever makes a kill will be the one that loses, leaving it to be a draw game. He goes back into the lounge area and says, "Teah, you know this is a draw game?"

"Yeah, I know."

"Then why do you keep insisting that I move?" he asks.

"Well, if you kill my man, I win. I was just waiting for you to make the kill, but now that you realize this was a useless game from the start, there is no reason to carry on. Fleece, have you ever wondered why chess, the most ancient game of all, has been kept around forever? I think it dates back to Earth."

The computer comes on and says, "That is correct. Chess was an ancient Earth development, a primitive way to improve IQ levels. This is the very reason it has been introduced to every star ship since its beginning. There is an ancient saying about the king and queen and each piece in the game, that the king and queen were empowered to run countries upon Earth."

"What exactly are countries?" Teah asks.

The computer answers, "Divided parts of land that governed groups of people would claim as their own and choose leaders over them, such as a king and queen which was later on changed to presidents and first ladies."

Teah asks the computer, "Did the first ladies rule the countries?"

The computer comes back and says, "Insufficient data."

Meanwhile, Tarvin continues to build onto his vessel using materials he has found on the planet as they have traveled. The vessel is more like a floating platform than an actual ship. Tarvin designed it this way to save time and materials. Since it doesn't rain where they are at, there seemed to be no reason to waste time building walls and a ceiling. Although after they were out of the danger zone, they did build rooms of a sort while leaving most of the platform to open air. This also solved their food problems as they can grow their food on the floating platform.

Heaps pass by quickly for them as they are constantly busy solving problems or inventing new ways to improve the vessel. As they travel, they eventually start to encounter other small groups of survivors, each of them having learned to survive the harsh environment in their own way. These survivors help build onto the platform, and at one time, their small community grows to around thirty survivors. Unfortunately, that doesn't last long as many lose their lives to planet tremors, predators, poisonous plants, and other dangers.

As Iniria grows older, she becomes more determined that there has to be more survivors out there. "The numbers just don't add up," she tells Tarvin as she develops a machine that can reach out to signals even on the other side of the planet.

One spot, she is working on the machine when she suddenly hears a voice boom over the radio, making her jump back in surprise. The voice continues to speak, saying something about a space station and obtaining parts for it. They continue on, unaware that Iniria is listening in. She can barely contain her excitement as she calls Tarvin over to listen.

After listening for a moment, his eyes wide, he asks her, "Can you locate the signal?"

Iniria nods, grinning with excitement, and fiddles with her data pad for a moment. Then, just as she is homing in the signal, it cuts off. "It's gone," she says, very disappointed.

"Wait! I've got something!" she yells after a moment. "It was somewhere in the northern hemisphere, but how can we get there?"

Tarvin gives her a hug as he grins from ear to ear. "You heard what they said, Little Bit. We can get off this planet," he says, determined. "We will find a way."

Chapter 7
Will the Tinidity Die?

They are now not far away from being finished with the star ship, the great space station, the Limonium. It is beautiful, twice the size of the previous star ship, three times lighter, and a hundred times stronger. A million times better with more resources than ever thought imaginable.

A lot of this is thanks to Tamia. Tamia has invented and discovered over a thousand different things on the planet. They harness every one of the heat stones they can. There are five of them, a heat source that is unquenchable. After rescuing the heat stones, she had went back into the canyon. It was no longer hot. There was ice on the walls, so she had to send up and get clothing suitable for cold weather. After they were all suited up, she went even farther into the canyon.

She took an ice pick and hit the wall. When she did, it shattered into a million pieces. Another great find. There is a small stone about the size of a gimmer, which is about two inches in diameter, frozen into the rock. It reads a constant temperature of thirty three and a half below zero. After a period of time, it builds up ice, creating an ice wall. There are about forty of these ice balls. Tamia calls them lantanite. You can use them for anything: refrigeration, air conditioning. It is just as great of a find as the heat stones were.

There is a plant discovered on the face of the planet called the Rolling Plant. It is about ten feet long and about the diameter of an average man's leg. It curls, spiraling outward. One end will bend on its spiraling end and work its way through the middle to the other end causing it to roll wherever it wants to go. The cool thing about this plant is that after taking the liquid out of it, you can put the lantanite in it and the cold will not penetrate through, creating a perfect mobile transport.

The last heap, just before the last shuttles are supposed to take off to the space station, Tamia is in a canyon with her team, excavating, looking for another discovery when the planet's tectonic plates move beneath the mountain they are on, causing a great shift in the two mountains. They both fall about ten feet, causing Tamia and her team to perish in the avalanche.

When the news of this is heard, there is great lamentation. Those that were closest to her were with her. There were twelve of them. There would have been fifteen, but three of her colleagues stayed on the space station to monitor the probes. This is how they found out the team was in the avalanche. It is a horrible loss! Some of the greatest minds of all times have perished these last several heaps.

Tamia's last discovery was a stone called tratite. It is very rare and very hard to get to, and it is only in the high mountains where Tamia and her team were. Now, after her death, the other scientists on the space station take the tratite and discover that they can make transporters that will actually move a person from one place to another instantaneously. Now, the development is on.

There is a young man named Botney. He latches onto these stones quickly and develops transporters throughout the ship, taking away the need altogether for elevators and stairways. It also provides means of surgery without cutting into the flesh. It can actually transport a tumor or cancer out of the body or transport veins to where new veins need to be and hold them there until it is mended. The stones are later called Tamia Stones because it was Tamia's greatest find.

Now, they can transport, but going light speed and transporting from one place to another is a total different thing. Botney and his team invent a ship transporter. They use Tamia stones to make a machine that will actually transport the ship one hundred light centuries away. They take one of the small ships, put it in front of the space station, and aim it toward the galaxy Rastour, unmanned. Then, they send it ahead. After five moments, they use the Tamia telescope to look for it. There it is. After setting the telemetry to where it should be, they can see that the ship is there and in perfect condition.

They setup a transporter booth on the ship where with accurate location and telemetry, they believe they can actually transport a person that far, from the space station to the ship that has been transported already. They have it all figured out. They will transport someone to the ship and then transport the ship back to the outside of the space station with the volunteer inside. Now, they just need a volunteer.

There is a young man named Damius Trethon, a smart young man. When he volunteers, some of the scientists are reluctant to send him. They do not want to lose one of their brightest young scientists. That's when he tells them, "I'm going."

Damius was one of the colleagues of Tamia that had stayed behind to monitor the probes. He was actually in love with her but had never told her this. He wants her greatest discovery to be revealed.

So, they do it. They transport him to the ship, not knowing anything, not sure what will happen. Damius has to calculate the transport back. He does, but he is a few thousand feet off, so he has to use conventional fuels, Now, he is ten feet off the bowel of the space station. They quickly radio over to his ship and ask him if everything went according to plan.

He says, "Yes, there was only one little problem. When the transporter transported me into the ship, the transporter area was clear, all except for a metal rod. Apparently during the first transport, the rod rolled off a piece of machinery, and the tip of it was in the transporter area. When I was transported into the ship, my fingers were transported into that rod, so I lost my last two fingers, or at least a part of them."

After Damius gets back to the station, they begin cybernetic surgery on his fingers and make them good as new. He is a hero, the first human to be transported to their knowledge. Because of the incident and such a high risk, the captain later on decides that the warping of humans at great distances will be forbidden until further technology is developed to ensure their safety. Now, with the developments and new planning and telemetry, they realize that reaching this faraway galaxy is only going to take around sixty heaps.

On the planet's surface, some of the colonators run into a real bad problem. One of the young girls is playing outside while her dad is planning and cultivating the garden. She notices in the ground that the dirt is stacking up by itself. It looks like a one inch tree, and then it will fall back down, move over a little bit, and do the same thing again.

She tells her dad about it, and he comes over to look. When it raises up the third time, he touches it. When he does, it mends itself to his fingernail, turning it black. It scares the life out of him. He quickly goes to the scientist that is head over that part of the colony.

The scientist's name is Ledor. Ledor is a very brilliant scientist.

He has doctorates that exceed his predecessors, and they were extremely smart, too. He takes the young girl's dad and leads him into the lab while the young girl holds onto her dad's other hand. He looks at the fingernail under a microscope.

When he does, he says to himself, "This is not good. Did your daughter touch this stuff?"

The man quickly answers, "No, I'm the only one that did."

That's when Mr. Ledor quickly says, "Quickly, come over here to the laser! I'm gonna try to laser cut it off and maybe kill the bacteria."

After lining up the man's finger with the laser and programming the laser to burn the stuff off of his fingernail, the laser moves backward and forward across his fingernail at light speed. Backward and forward, up and down. Two or three times, it goes across. The fingernail is no longer black. It has turned a reddish color.

Ledor takes him back over to the microscope and looks at it again. The only thing that has happened is that it has changed colors. The stuff turned red, and then it turns back to black. But as he continues to look at it under the microscope, he sees that it isn't covering the man's fingernail, but it is actually dissolving his fingernail and taking its place. The cells are splitting, and each time they split, it dissolves a little more. Now time wise, it has been a couple of moments. Ledor figures out that if it has doubled and dissolved his fingernail and part of his finger in a couple of moments, then in another couple of moments, it will have dissolved twice that.

Quickly, he gets on conference with other scientists and lets them know what is happening. They quarantine the gentleman quickly, putting him in a room beside the lab. Now inside the room, there is medical equipment, and the room is able to kill any germ or bacteria. Ledor lets the other scientists know that he has tried to burn the stuff off the finger with no effect. That's when fear strikes the scientists. Because now, the cells are splitting even faster, and then even faster, and then every few seconds. Now, the tip of his finger is black.

The man begins to go into cardiac arrest because of fear. There is a cybernetic android that has been developed and is able to stay in the room and doctor on the gentleman. The android tries to cut off the man's finger to do further lab analysis but it cannot be penetrated. By this time, his whole hand is black, and it is starting to move up his arm.

After the man goes into cardiac arrest, the android which is called Z123, quickly revives him by injecting him with adrenaline. After that, he sedates him so that he will remain calm. "Are you in any pain?" Z123 asks.

"No," the man answers, "but cut my arm off!"

As soon as the android hears the man tell him to cut his arm off, he quickly puts him over to where he can do laser surgery. By this time, the black stuff has moved up past his elbow. Z123 quickly responds, saying, "We must hurry. At this rate, you will not be alive long."

As quickly as possible, he uses the laser to cut through the man's arm. They put it into a containment booth which is about three feet in diameter and about six feet long. They watch it consume the rest of the arm. While observing the arm, they try to penetrate it with a laser. After about fifteen moments of not being able to do anything to it, it just melts away into microscopic dust. After tending to the man with no arm, they still have him in quarantine just to make sure he is alright.

Meanwhile, the little girl had went back to get her mom. Ledor and the others hear a horrible scream. They run as quickly as they can. The little girl is standing there, screaming, horrified at what she just saw. Her mother had been out in the garden for a while. The plants were quite high, so no one knew that she had touched the stuff, too, before her husband. She is now just a black statue, standing there, looking at her hand. Apparently, when the stuff got on her hand, she had went into shock, not being able to move. While they are looking at her, the mom falls to the ground, nothing but microscopic dust.

That's when terror strikes the whole colony. The statues of people are being found everywhere if they haven't already turned to dust. There are several of them. They quickly quarantine the colony, putting them on their ships.

Ledor calls this stuff Tinidity. It is a horrible disease. Although it is as rare as it can be, it is more deadly than any virus or bacteria known to man. The Tinidity goes away as fast as it came, but not before fear strikes through all the land. Everybody is afraid to touch the dirt from that spot on. Ledor, himself, goes to the space station and refrains from going back to the face of the planet after that. There are a few families that choose to stay on the surface, but he is against it because of this episode.

There have been a few other episodes where people died on the planet. Like one of the most beautiful flowers, when a woman went to pick it, the microscopic hairs on the stem of it stuck into her finger. It was a horrible death. Everywhere she touched, it transferred those microscopic thorny-like needles and pretty soon after three quarters of a sector as she touched her face and then touched her hands, she was completely in pain because of the needle pricking thorns all over her. They kept duplicating and breaking off. Every time she touched somewhere, it would make more thorns, and every one of them were real tiny.

They called this cactunite, the most beautiful flower and the most deadly. She died in horrible pain. Each prick of the cactunite was like a really, really bad stinging creature bite, and there were thousands of them. Each time she transferred a touch to her body, she screamed in agonizing pain.

By the time they had figured out a cure for the cactunite, she had already perished, within a sector. Had she survived one quarter of a sector more, they could have gotten completely rid of it. The cure is in the flower's leaves that grow out of the stem. Apparently, all you have to do is rub the leaf on the part the cactunite touched, and the thorn-like hairs will stick to the leaf and not duplicate anymore. They were able to wipe the lady's face, hands, and everywhere she had touched off and prepare her for burial without the cactunite all over her.

The rate of birth these last few heaps has drastically increased. Every family produces anywhere from six to twenty children. This moves the population up quite a bit. Some of the children perish before reaching the age of five. That's when it is decided that all children should move to the space station unless their parents insist otherwise. The planet's hostility is too volatile for the children and sometimes even for the adults. Every family knows that they have to colonize the new planet, and to do this, they will have to have plenty of children. Some of the scientists have children. If the parents are strong, the children are stronger. If the parents are smart, the children are smarter.

For some reason, the oxygen on the planet increases their metabolism, and because the air is so pure, ninety nine percent of the time, the brain is able to be accessed at its full potential, causing people to be smarter, stronger, faster, and able to do things for a longer period of time. A two sector workload is no more; now they are able to work seven sectors straight through, around the spot.

Fleece and Teah had expected to reach the surface leans ago. Unfortunately, the cliff they were climbing had widened out, so they had to go back down and wait for it to go back up again. By this time, the robotic arm, for some reason, started working again. Apparently, some of the goo had gotten clogged up in it, and after moving around for a heap, it had unclogged. Now, the computer comes up and says, "We are at the end of our ascent and are approaching the surface.

That's when the command is given to de-cryogenilize the other three. After Que and Serena are awake and have their passionate moment together, Que says the thing that they ought to do is come up just a little bit to where the analyzing probe compartment is and check the temperature to see if it is safe to come up all at once.

They all agree, and as the vessel enters into the atmosphere, the compartment door is opened just a tad. The solar blast of the sun heats it up to ten thousand degrees. They immediately go back down. Five inches from the surface is where the top of their ship is now, and the temperature levels out. They realize the material they are in can withstand any type of heat or any type of cold. This is an amazing discovery.

They go back down for another two leans then come back up just enough to take another reading. The computer shuts it down and brings them back under, saying that the heat peaked the thermometer. It is at one hundred thousand degrees. It burns the thermometer up, so they estimate that they were at the peak and it will take three or four more leans before they can actually enter upper atmosphere.

By then, it is coming into the seventh heap. Being full term in pregnancy by now, Serena and Que decide they do not want to have their baby underground so they go back into cryogenics, but unfortunately they are woken not long after because of a

111

malfunction and do not go back into cryogenics after that. It is time. Serena is due. After Que places her in a medical pod, she has a healthy young boy by the name of Cadum.

Four leans later, after seven years and two leans underground, they come up out of the ground. They are so happy to be on the surface. "But where are all the other ships?" they wonder among themselves.

Que asks the computer if the planet is inhabitable. The computer comes back and says, "Air is stable. Gravity is stable. Life support is stable."

One by one, they exit the ship. Although the robotic arms on the outside of the ship are massive in size, their tips are worn down about a foot. The tracks extend out beneath the ship, and the computer lays out a course and plots the telemetry that it needs to stay out of the hot, scorching sun. There is a ship on the side of one of the cliffs that looks like it has gone through the solar blasts several times. It is melted into the side of the cliff. What isn't melted is hardly recognizable. There is no one.

After several heaps go by, Commander Alexander realizes he can live on board indefinitely as long as he continues to recycle his resources, the energy source on board lasts, and nothing happens to the ship's primary resources, such as life support. Exhausted, he can't stop thinking about his brother and sister and wondering if his mom, dad, and the rest of his family ever made it to the new planet.

Now, another heap has gone by. The commander has now given up hope. That's when good news comes over the computer, "The Y2DB solar system is now in view, and we are approximately two heaps from reaching the paradise belt planet's orbit."

He thinks to himself, "Seven heaps of being up here alone."

"Quickly, see if you can establish radio communication," he tells the computer.

The computer comes back and says, "Commander, I have been trying to establish communication the whole time. We have tried several frequencies. We are continually scanning the frequencies, but we have received no response as of yet. I will keep trying." The commander even gets on the radio himself occasionally to see if he can find a frequency that someone might be using.

The commander is not a religious man, but before he lays down to go to sleep each spot, he thinks to himself, "Oh God, if you are there, I am so tired of being alone."

Now it has been a very stressful seven heaps for Commander Alexander, being lost in space and trying to find his way back to where the Planeterial crashed. He is now almost there, almost back into the solar system. After a couple of very stressful sectors, he lies down and falls asleep. Little does he know, this spot is different.

He has a dream. He is in a field of coffee, and as he is walking through it, he begins to float.

Then, people start to float up out of the coffee beans, and they are smiling at him. "You're not alone. Look!" they say as they point at someone at the end of the coffee.

Then, the likeness of a young beautiful woman floats up out of the end of the coffee. She says, "Here I am! Here I am! I have been here all along."

After waking up soaking wet with sweat, he thinks to himself, "What a pleasant dream, even though it was paranormal like." He shakes his head as he gets ready to start a new spot of time. He wraps a towel around his waist as he always does and steps into the shower.

Now the shower is quite elaborate. On one side, it has the

lavatory, and on the other side, it has the showers. There are four in a row. As with every shuttle, there is a backup of three or four lavatories and everything in it. If one thing goes down, you have the others to fall back on until it is fixed. There are three ways into the shower. There is one way from one captain's quarters and one from the other, and then there is a maintenance entrance that comes in on the north side for the android to come in and maintain the facilities.

After entering into the shower, he hears water running and thinks maybe one of the showers is broken. Just when he hears the shower water running, it stops. He steps around just in time for a young woman to step out, and there they are, staring each other face to face.

During the commander's dream, there is a cryogenic pod that is counting down to an expiration date. Five hundred and twelve heaps, five sectors, and thirty moments.

Three, two, one...

De-cryogenics begin. It is a young, beautiful woman. She has been in cryogenics for over five hundred heaps. The pod slides out of a compartment, and the seals break after the liquid is absorbed out of the pod. Her tubes are removed, and her lungs are cleared. Resuscitation has begun. After a few moments, she begins to breathe on her own.

After taking in a few deep breaths, she sits up on the side of the pod. Her legs hang down over the pod beside her name plate. Right beside the computer panel, it reads, "Woodlynn Lafi."

After sitting there several moments, she realizes that her unclothed body is still sticky from the thealopium gel. She holds onto the pod as she steps down to the floor, holding herself up very carefully. She steps into the shower room, and as soon as she steps up onto the panel, the shower begins to rinse her off.

As they look at each other face to face, the commander thinks to himself, "I am seeing things." His heart almost faints.

When Woodlynn sees the commander and how white he looks, she says, "Are you okay? Sir? Are you okay?"

The commander takes in a deep breath. He can hardly speak the words. "How is it possible? How are you on this ship?"

"You mean the captain's space shuttle, in case something happens to the Planeterial? Well, that's easy to explain. I'm the captain's daughter. Why are you here? Are we there?"

"There?" the commander asks. "What do you mean, there? Where is there?"

"At our destination, the new planet," she replies. "What's going on? Tell me the update. And where's my dad? Where's everybody at?"

"You've been in cryogenics all this time? I've been all over this shuttle. I did not see a cryo-pod that was being used, not one with anyone in it. I guess I should have been a little more observant. Apparently, there was one."

"What is the date?" she asks. She is beginning to get worried.

After the commander tells her the heap, she says, "That's impossible! Five hundred and thirteen heaps! I've been asleep five hundred and thirteen heaps! I was supposed to be woke up a couple of hundred heaps ago. The maximum time it was supposed to take to get to the planet was three hundreds heaps."

"Where's my dad?" she demands frantically.

"I'm afraid I have bad news." The commander isn't sure how to tell her. "Captain Lafi, well...Captain Lafi...well, there was an accident."

She sits down on a bench beside the commander. As she turns

her head and looks at him, quivering, with a sobering voice, she asks, "What happened?"

"There were several gamma blasts from a nearby solar system. He went to check on navigations, and one of the blasts went through the navigation room. He was sucked out into space. He never knew what happened."

"Why wasn't I woke up?" she says, not believing what she is hearing.

"Well, the ship went into red alert, and it was destroyed completely. I suppose the captain assumed everybody was de-cryogenilized when the emergency de-cryogenics kicked in. Apparently, among all the malfunctions, the link up to this ship's communications were down. Apparently, they were going to take this ship, but when they realized communications were down, they left in another ship. There was another ship just like this one. During the panic, you must have been totally overlooked, and so was I. Since there was no link up to the computer, nobody knew you were in cryogenics," he explains. That's when the commander begins to feel sick inside, almost to the point of throwing up, thinking about how there has been somebody here the whole time.

As she grabs the towel that is wrapped around her and stands to her feet, she tries to grab her wits about her as she goes into her room and begins to get dressed. She can't believe what she has just heard.

After the commander quickly gets through with the facilities and gets dressed, he comes into the other captain's quarters where Woodlynn is now dressed and about to come out. "We may be the only two people left," he tells her.

Horrified and scared, he puts his arms around her. She puts her head on his chest and says, "I'm scared."

The commander, not knowing how to comfort her or what to

116

say at first, finally speaks."I was a lot more terrified before you were here."

"What do you mean?" she asks as she pulls away from his chest.

"I've been alone for seven heaps," he answers.

"Oh, you poor dear," she says as she looks into his face and her eyes bottle up with tears. She can only think to herself how horrible that must have been. No one to speak to. And as she thinks to herself, she could be alone right now, she begins to sigh silently as the commander continues.

He says, "I've been trying to navigate back to the planet where the escape shuttles went. I have radio communications back up. It took me heaps to do it."

"Why did it take so long?"

"Well, I took every bus apart that linked to the computer, the navigations, the communications, life support. I went through every one of them, but on the communications board, the bus and everything checked out positive. It was great. The analyzer analyzed it. Nothing was wrong, not one thing. I spent two heaps going over it time after time, hundreds of times. Every time I put the computer bus card back in its slot, everything seemed to be okay, except for one thing. The little plastic piece on the far end, farthest from me on the opposite side, had broken off the clip and went down into the bus slot, keeping the card from going into the bus slot and keeping the pins from connecting which caused the communication failure. It was only about a sixteenth of an inch, but it was just enough to keep the pins from connecting.

I never would have noticed. I accidentally ran across it after pulling out each bus card hundreds of times, but this last time, I pulled two of them at the same time. And as I was about to put one back into its slot, I looked at the back, at the clips. They looked identical, except the shadow from the light I was shining on them cast a different shadow. I moved the light to the second one where the differential was, and I began to say to myself, 'Well, that wouldn't stop this bus from working.' So I got a mirror and looked down in the bus, and that's when I saw the little plastic piece down in there. Apparently, somebody had tried to take the bus out without releasing the clip, and the card cut the little clip in it off. When it did, it fell into the slot. Well, to make a long story short..."

"Yeah, two heaps long," she says.

"Exactly," the commander replies. "Communications are now fixed. I was able to add in some new frequencies, trying to reach farther away to see if I can gather up any information of anybody being alive or not. So far, I have been unsuccessful. It is so good to be talking to somebody. I've been talking to a computer for heaps now. I've navigated a course back, but unfortunately, I don't know how to get any closer. The computer says if we get any closer, the solar energy from this sun will burn us up."

On the Limonium, there are now close to fifteen hundred people not including the people on the planet. None of them want to return to the surface. It is near time to depart.

It was voted that Ronson was the more knowledgeable about maintenance and morale of people. And since he was primarily the second smartest scientist, outside of his younger brother, who didn't want the job of captain in the first place, they decided it would be best for Ronson to be the leader and captain of the vessel.

Eleven hundred people are put into cryogenics. Some have been there for a heap or two, testing the new gel, but they are awakened for this special event. Some will only be woke up if something utopic happens, and that's highly likely. There are about one hundred and fifty people preparing for the warp. They are all excited.

There are over one hundred people that want to stay on the planet. Even some of the top scientists refuse to leave. No matter how much they insist for them to leave, they insist they will stay. There are twenty-five ships left on the planet's surface that automatically move when they are supposed to. With a constant climate change, plants, animals, everything changes heap round. It can go from bad to worse or from good to better. For the most part, until now, it has stayed the same. One heap, it was really good. The next, it was really bad. Anything from freezing winters to blistering summers. But just like life on planet Earth once was, it's their way of life.

On the Limonium, everybody radios down to the face of the planet to say their goodbyes. They will never see them again. If they don't go now, they will be on the planet forever. At the last moment, twenty-five people change their mind. The thought of the ship leaving without them, well...they just can't take the stress of it.

As soon as their ships are locked into the space station, Captain Ronson gives the order, "Prepare for space transportation."

Soon, the spot is at hand, and now everybody is ready for the warp. All of the magnetic propulsion systems are turned on. Lasers are shot in front of the ship. All calculations are made. All the force fields are turned on. Everybody has to get in a space suit because they do not know what to expect. A lot of other safety precautions are taken. This will be the first time they have tried to warp a station of this size. Before a space warp, there has to be a trajectory cleanse. In the trajectory cleanse, it consists of the warp drive warping every piece of space dust out of its pathway because like the rod in Damius' finger, anything warped into stays at its present location.

Captain Ronson is eager to be on the way. After conversing

with his brother and going through the ship checking every area for the last two rests, he and his brother, Corton, decide that it is time to take the warp drive into trans-warp. He is in continual contact with the warp room. On each suit, they have an intercom system. All they have to do is talk. It is all computerized. He can say a name, and it will instantly broadcast to the frequency of their suit. When the captain speaks, everybody's suit hears the captain speaking, unless he says a particular name, and then it is solo between the two.

He gives the command to Darlene, who is in charge of the warp room, to get the warp drive up to its maximum capacity. She turns to the one in control of the warp drive to maintain its stability, increase its power, and activate its warp process. She gives her the order to bring it up slowly. They each one enter into a small room outside of the warp drive room with a layer of littonite, a glass-like material created from the resources on this planet. From here, they watch the warp drive as it starts glowing, as the discs start to spin faster.

At first, one thousand RPMs, then ten thousand, then one hundred thousand. When it reaches one million RPMs, it is at its maximum capacity. After that, it reaches its non-readable capacity and begins to glow where you cannot see it anymore.

As the radio frequency gets higher, Darlene measures its frequencies very carefully to make sure everything is perfect. E.X., a seismographic scientist that works with her, measures the tremors of the ship. At maximum power, it is at a hum. You can barely hear it. No seismic activity hardly at all outside of the sixty million hertz frequency that it puts out. It is barely measurable.

After about ten moments, Darlene relays the message, saying, "Captain, we are all good here. All the readings are normal. We are ready when you are."

There is a helm in the captain's booth. The helmsman is the one who actually puts the station into warp. When all is in place, the captain gives the command to the helmsman. "Warp," he yells out.

Chapter 8
Alone At Last

Doc Husby's family is one of the families that chose to stay on the planet. Mr. Husby is a pretty inspirational man. Everybody knows him and likes him. He isn't one to bark out orders, but everybody looks to him as a supervisor, so to speak. If they have questions, he is the one they go to. His close friends call him DD, in short for Doctor Doc.

Now, DD is also short for Daddy which all three of his children call him. It is sort of honorary, constructed by his fifteen heap old, who was seven when they landed on this planet. He said, "Dad, you know, everybody calls you DD, and I call you Dad. I think it will only be honorary for me to take the 'A' out. If that's okay with you, I am going to call you DD from now on. Doctor Doc for others and Dad for us, or if you'd rather, I'll call you Pop."

"No, no, DD's fine."

It didn't go over at first with the other siblings, but after Brittle kept calling him DD, the others just got into the habit of it by mistake even though they objected to it from the start. Trina is now married and doesn't see her dad that often, so the DD didn't stick with her like it did the other two.

Now, Doc and his wife stand there as the others disappear from the planet, including some of Doc's closest friends. He can't help but to cry as they leave. When Mrs. Husby sees him crying, she breaks down, too. That's when it hits the others. We're here alone.

That's when everybody starts to sob.

Doc Husby says, "I don't know if we made the right choice."

That's when one of his friends who stayed behind with him, Mr. Traylon, says, "Listen Doc, you made the right choice, along with the rest of us. We're doing a good thing here. We've got a good stable home and a good life. And we don't have to go into cryogenics, spending our whole life looking for a planet that we may never find. Besides that, you don't even know if the Limonium is going to make it to a planet. Look what happened to the Planeterial. It was destroyed, along with a lot of my friends and family, including my mom and dad, along with your mom and dad, too. Don't forget that, DD"

"Yeah, you're right," he says. "I still can't help but to feel the pain of the loss of those that left. It's almost like a part of me left with them."

That's when Mr. Traylon's daughter says, "Who knows? Maybe we will see them again or pick them up on an odd frequency. You know I'm in charge of radio communications."

After she makes things light hearted, everybody's morale begins to pick back up. That's when everybody scatters out to go back to work.

Now, one of the families that stayed behind are complete adrenaline addicts. The biggest reason they stayed was because of the Paladeus Canyons, the one hundred mile fall straight down. Beckor dives two or three times a spot during the season of the great canyon. Being how it only lasts a few rests out of the heap that they can actually get to it safely without being in the blistering cold or scorching heat, they take double advantage of it. A round trip down and back takes about a sector, but this time it is different for Beckor.

This dive, he sees at the bottom that there is a strange set of lights, rotating blue lights that appear to be green until he gets closer. It isn't green lights at all. It is a set of blue lights on top of a disc with a set of yellow lights on the bottom of it, making it appear green.

Reluctant to take off back to the surface, he keeps on free falling until it gets closer. "Is it an alien?" he thinks to himself. "Or some kind of prehistoric being from another planet. Or maybe it's monsters," he thinks. "Or maybe the fall itself is causing me to hallucinate."

The excitement is overwhelming, seeing this on top of the adrenaline flowing through his veins at one hundred percent. A couple of miles up, that's when the platform levitates upward. There are three people on it, and they are in space suits.

That's when Beckor thinks to himself, "They look like us. Could it be maybe they've come through time? Maybe they came from our past?"

As he gets closer and they take their helmets off, a young beautiful woman catches his eye. That's when he turns on his jet packs and stops right where he is at. Then, he slowly descends to where they are. They are looking straight at him.

Then he speaks, "Do you speak English?"

That's when Iniria busts out laughing. She says to her brother, "Don't let him know we speak English."

Tarvin starts walking like a robot and says, "Yes... we... speak... English...," very slowly and robotically.

When Beckor sees and hears this, he turns white, flies up to the top as quick as possible, and hurries to tell the others about what he has seen. The first person he runs into is a woman, Mrs. Baldren, and her little boy. "What's wrong with you? You look like you've seen a ghost," she asks.

"There's someone at the bottom."

That's when her son says, "Oh, another practical joke. Ha Ha Ha."

He quickly runs past Mrs. Baldren and her son and runs to the others. Now Beckor is all the time trying to get people to jump, and he is all the time scheming, trying to trick people to jump off the edge just so they can feel what he feels. He comes to DD in haste. He says, "DD, come to the bottom of the canyon! There are people down there on some kind of alien vessel!"

But this time, he has cried wolf too many times DD will not even turn around and look at him as he has done this before when he pulls his practical jokes. That's when Beckor steps in front of DD, and when DD sees his face and sees how white as a ghost he is and how he is shaking from head to toe, he figures he better go check into this. But this time, he gets several laser armed androids, and they get a team together and go down to the platform.

Upon arriving, Tarvin, his sister, and one of the other crew are still waiting on their platform. That's when Tarvin realizes that his practical prank may have went too far when he sees laser armed androids come down. They put their arms up in the air and say, "We are friendly."

That's when Iniria says, "We come in peace."

Tarvin busts out laughing and says, "Are you gonna give it a break yet?"

That's when DD realizes that it is survivors. As he listens to their conversation, he can't help but to laugh, too. After introducing himself to Tarvin and some of the others, they tell them all that has happened and what they are doing now. They all get on the platform and raise up to the surface.

Now, Que and Serena's son, Cadum grew very fast. His eye was on the young scientist, Teah, his constant companion and mentor. Now Teah is almost twenty-five by the time Cadum makes it to ten heaps old, and she never ceases to amaze him in everything they converse in. By the time he is sixteen, he has already grown to full size, and he is terribly in love with Teah. Now Teah being a little over thirty heaps old now, never thinks about anything besides crunching numbers and has no idea how Cadum really feels about her.

By this time, Cadum has several brothers and sisters. Serena, after being introduced to the planet's atmosphere, conceived again and again. She had two girls and a boy the first time, three boys and two girls the second time, and now she is pregnant with six children. With several children running around and able to help with chores, Cadum is the leader of most of them and somewhat of a good mentor, along with Teah and Fleece, the only other two there.

Now Trim Breville had been with them. He was the first scientist off the ship. He did not trust the computer's analysis. Matter of fact, he didn't trust anybody or anything. If he didn't see it, touch it, or analyze it with his own hands and eyes, he did not trust it. He did not believe it. Very arrogant and very untrustworthy. Mainly because he didn't trust anybody, nobody trusted him.

Now being the first into cryogenics proved his lack of interest in the crew or their survival. Teah, on the other hand, had realized that the food resources would be more adequate if they were in hibernation. This was not so with Trim. Although he was a very good analyst, he was not a very good person at all. To what his motivation was, the other four had no idea. Although he did his job and did it well, he was arrogant toward everyone else's work. He wasn't any better than anybody else in his work but always had a snobby look when anybody accomplished anything. He didn't have to say much for them to realize that he was a snob.

126

Being the first one off the ship in his space suit, he explored the terrain. Before he left, Teah said, "Mr. Breville, don't go too far. We need to stay in close contact."

He turned around with his space helmet looking toward her and gave her a spiteful look, as if he didn't need a mother or something, especially one so young.

Trim kept walking for a distance, and after about a quarter of a sector of exploring, he got very tired and very sleepy. That's when he decided he would sit down for a moment in between two stumps. He leaned his back up against one of the stumps which was about two feet off the ground. When he did, he fell fast asleep.

Now, after a sector, not realizing that the oxygen supply was getting low, he remained in a deep sleep. That's when Teah told Serena, "Shouldn't Mr. Breville be back by now? He did have his suit on, but the oxygen supply should be low."

That's when Fleece said, "Oh, surely he had enough wits about him to take off his helmet by now. I wouldn't worry about him, Teah."

Que told Fleece, "Maybe we should go look for him, just in case."

Fleece said, "Well, I've really got a lot to do. I don't think we ought to worry about him. He would find it absurd for us to look for him anyway." Everybody knew this was the truth about Mr. Breville, knowing his personality and all.

"If he isn't back in a while, we will go look for him, but right now, we need to establish how we are going to survive on this planet," Fleece continued.

The other three agreed, but after a short while, they all began to wonder. He should have been back. That's when Fleece and Que decided to go ahead and look for him anyway.

His footsteps were on the ground very plain to see for a long while, but after a quarter sector of following them, they decided to sit down for a moment. After articulating for several moments and getting their breath, Que said, "I wonder where he went."

That's when Fleece looked over behind where Que was sitting and saw Trim laying up against the stump. "There he is, right there," he said.

They quickly went over. He appeared to be asleep at first. They slid his helmet off. He had been dead for a quarter sector now. After seeing his suit's regulator on empty, Fleece said, "He suffocated?!? With all this oxygen, he suffocated?!?"

Que couldn't say anything. He just shook his head backward and forward. They couldn't say they didn't feel anything for him, because they did, especially since there were only six people left on the planet, as far as they knew. And now, one was dead.

After recovering his body and preparing him, they buried Trim Breville in the sinking sand, which was not sand at all.

That's when Serena said, "It's ironic. Isn't it?"

"What?" Que asked.

"He didn't want to contribute to helping us get out and wanted to sleep while we were in the sand. Now, we're burying him in it, and he will be asleep in it forever."

Que says, "Serena!"

"Well, Que, it's true. He wasn't a very good person, and I'm very sad to see him go in such a horrible way."

After she thought about what she had said, she couldn't help but to cry as she felt sorry for saying it, even though she knew it was true and the others did, also.

After a while on the planet, they came up with the idea that they could use this sand substance to make houses with. Although they couldn't live in them heap round, they could go back to living in them when the solar blasts from the sun passed and they came back around which was really cool because they didn't have to build new houses. So, every three leans, they would build a new house and just move from house to house. They were learning to survive on the harsh planet's surface. But they still wondered what had happened to everyone else.

After several leans of the commander and Woodlynn getting to know each other and getting more familiar with the ship, Woodlynn comes up with an idea. She puts her idea on the display and says, "Commander, look at this. This planet does not spin, at least not noticeably. I've been observing it, and the only way they could have made it and be out of the solar blasts would have been to get around this ring here."

She begins to explain more as she points at the diagram. "In a few leans, this planet will be directly in front of the solar system. That's when we can navigate to one side or the other of this belt and stay on one side or the other away from the solar heat of the sun."

Now Dr. Woodlynn is very familiar with trajectory, telemetry, and navigation. Matter of fact, she was the head of her class three to one. She isn't just a smart person. She knows how to use it, able to apply every little mathematical equation to its job and duty.

Commander Alexander knew the captain, Woodlynn's dad, very well. The commander was next in line to be captain on the Planeterial. First, you became second captain, and then you became first captain. He was first commander, in line to be second captain. The first commander was under the first captain, Captain Lafi. The second commander was under the second captain.

Captain Lafi had talked about his daughter many times, but he had never mentioned that he had her in cryogenics. He always talked as if she was on the ship somewhere. He had woken up three times during the five hundred heap flight and been put back into cryogenics. Each commander was woke up every seventy five heaps. One was woke, and then seventy five heaps later, the other was woke. They stayed up for five heaps, along with the captain, and served only under the captain that was on hand. The captains did the same, keeping the same commander and the same captain each shift. So, every seventy-five heaps, they alternated their five heap rounds. The androids monitored the ship during the time between the captain's rounds, so if there was something wrong, the captains would be woke up, which was how Woodlynn's dad was awake.

As the commander thought about this, he told Woodlynn, "From the captain's log, you and I should have been woken up. There is an entry in there where your dad gave the command to the computer to de-cryogenilize us and all the upper staff. Apparently, the command was abated because of the communications failure."

"How did you end up with captain's log?" she asks.

"I'm not really sure," the commander replies. "His personal computer log had been updated from the other ship and everything that happened. Apparently, he had put it down in his quarters. After finding out the communications were out in this ship, apparently, he had forgotten and left it there. Maybe it was because they were in such a big hurry, but that's where I got the coordinates to where the escape shuttles landed."

"Why was my dad chosen to be woke up instead of the other captain?"

"After one captain is put in cryogenics, anything that happens after that, the other captain's shift kicks in automatically. The other captain was put in cryogenics not long before something happened to the warp drive and put the ship off course for two hundred heaps. Had your dad not been woken up and canceled warp speed, we would have crashed right into the star......," he explains.

What they don't know is that two hundred heaps earlier, some of the maintenance crew of the Planeterial were de-cryogenilized. It was a simple process. Every computer component was diagnosed from three different teams. Each team had six people on it. There were eighteen people in all. After one team tested each component for navigation, communication, life support, the other team would do the same. Likewise, the third team.

In the captain's emergency space shuttle, Que Bounty was one of the technicians overseeing the analyzation of each component. The first team did the first run. The second team did the second run, and the third team did the third run. Now, Que, being at the end of the third team, oversaw the finalization of all the runs.

Now Que's hands were a little bigger than the rest of the team, and his first finger, for some reason, had been getting numb. So, when he lifted some of the bus cards up from the back and unclipped them with his first finger on his left hand, some of them he couldn't feel. Having big hands made him a little stronger, so when he lifted the bus card up, it broke the pin off the clip that holds the card in. After checking the card, he put it back in the bus, but it didn't sink properly.

On his way out of the ship, the computer analyzed the communications. As soon as he walked out, the door shut, and the computer was saying, "Communications Failure. Communications Failure."

Now, navigations was the last part to be checked over. As usual, each team did its process, and now Que Bounty was about to do his finalization as he had done on the captain's shuttle. Now the space station was a little different although it had the same setup. Even though the cards were different and the components on them were made different, it still had the same process of hooking it to the bus. These parts were designed where they would not wear out unless they were mishandled. On the main circuit board, there were seventy-five buses. Seventy of the cards were about two feet long, three inches high. There was another bus on the side of each one of those cards that another set of cards plugged into. There was also a set of conventional wire ribbons hooked to the secondary card that ran off the primary card.

Now when navigations and telemetry were plotted, each card had its processing unit to do a specific thing. This particular card processed the time that the ship would travel on the telemetry it was set on. When Que disconnected the primary wiring from the secondary card and unplugged it, the same type of clip broke the same way. Only this time, the little plastic piece fell inside the female end of the plug-in, the gold plated copper connection to the female plug-in. When he plugged it back up, the plastic piece was underneath the back part of it. So, the gold pin that plugged into it only connected a fraction of an inch to the female plug. When the card was re-engaged, it appeared that there was nothing wrong.

Analyzing with the computer, the card and its bus appeared to be okay, but when Que went to shut the drawer that all the cards were connected to, it caused the connection to break two or three times in a fraction of a second, causing the time of arrival to pass up by two hundred heaps. Que, not knowing what he had done, and the computer analyzing it like it was a new entry had no idea that there was something wrong. Until two hundred heaps later when the ship's trajectory was heading straight for a star.

This is the reason the captain was woken up. The other captain had just went back into cryogenics just before the ship's trajectory was put off course. No one was woken up for the shifts during the two hundred heap overshot.

Captain Lafi wakes up with the sound of the computer saying, "Captain, we are on a collision course with a star that is going supernova in the Y2DB galaxy, the Sheelsium solar system."

"Quick, take us out of warp!"

"De-warping now, Captain. Unfortunately, we are in the gravitational pull of the Sheelsium sun."

"Can we break away from it?"

"I am pulling resources as we speak. Rocket fuel down to thirteen percent. We are re-routing ten percent of the space shuttles' fuel to the main rocket engines."

"Why do we have to use conventional rocket fuel? Use impulse engines, nuclear fusion. Use anything."

"Captain, it's going to take all that and rocket fuel to pull away from this solar system's gravitational pull."

"Are you going to be able to handle it?"

"Yes, fortunately, it is all under control."

The captain quickly takes a shower and gets dressed, and as he usually does on his shift, he takes a walk and goes to the scientific department. As the captain walks into the scientific department, he feels as if this is the end of his time. It is as if he knows his long lived life is somewhat coming to an end.

As he gets to the cryogenics department in the scientific lab, he comes to the pod and looks over a young beautiful woman named Glyria. He is terribly in love with her. He pauses for a moment as he looks at each feature on her face. He knows his time of waking was not yet supposed to be, so he ponders for a moment whether to wake Glyria up as he has before. They have a very passionate love affair, and he can't wait to tell his daughter about her.

So, he slides his finger across the panel, and the little red button lights up. Hesitant to mash the red button that appears on the screen, he wonders to himself whether he should or not, but longing to hold her, he can't stand it. He mashes the button.

Just then, the computer comes over the intercom. "Captain, quick! There are gamma blasts from the inner core of the galaxy. There seems to be something wrong in navigations."

On the way into navigations, the captain gives the computer the order to wake Commander Alexander, his daughter Woodlynn, and the rest of the upper level of command. As he gets into the room, the computer says, "Communication to the main captain's shuttle has been breached."

As soon as the computer says that, a gamma blast comes up through the floor right through the navigations computer and right out through the hull of the ship. It is a perfect one foot hole. The captain is sucked right through it. There is nothing left of him.

The commander and Woodlynn spend several leans navigating to the paradise belt planet and laying down plans to land and establish communication with everyone, if there is anyone there. That's when the computer picks up radio communication with some of those on the planet.

The commander says, "Quickly, establish a link!"

"Link already established, Commander."

There is a young girl on the radio frequency by the name of Suslyn. Now Suslyn is a young thirteen heap old girl who has an average IQ level of six hundred. She dreads this dreadful planet, has never liked it. Her little scientific mind can only think of the wonders of the cosmos and the exploration of the cosmos. She longs to travel through space, and after many leans of developing communications throughout the paradise belt, she constantly monitors to see if she can get a hold of the Limonium.

But on this particular spot of time, she is reluctant to get on the radio at all, thinking to herself, "This is a waste of time." Being head of communications at thirteen heaps old, even that proves to be boredom most of the time. But this spot will be terribly different. Her usefulness will be proven after all these long leans of radio communication.

That's when it happens. She is speaking to one of the techs that is on an expedition when she loses communication with them. Scanning through the frequencies, she keeps saying, "Hello, are you there? What happened? I've lost communication with you."

After trying several new frequencies, she decides to try an old frequency that she has not tried in a long time. "Hello? Can anybody hear me?"

When the commander hears her voice, he says, "Hello, this is Commander Alexander, captain's ship of the Planeterial!"

She says, "Hello, this is Suslyn. Is this some kind of trick? I am head of communications. I know everyone's voice. I've never heard yours. I also know there is no captain's ship or any ship outside of the twenty-five that were left here and those we have found."

"Man, I am so glad to hear your voice," he tells her. "We have been trying to establish communication with the survivors. I have been lost in space for eight heaps."

Suslyn gets so excited. Okay, she gets more than excited. Matter of fact, she gets hysterical and starts bouncing around all over the place. "Dad, Dad, quickly!" she yells, but her dad does not hear her.

She says, "Wait a moment! Let me get my dad." Before she can hardly get it out of her mouth, she is halfway out the door.

She runs to where her dad is standing with a group of people surrounding him including DD. She says, "Dad, come quickly! There's a ship in our solar system! It's from the Planeterial!"

He looks at her puzzled and says, "Just a moment, Suslyn. I'm in the middle of a discussion."

She grabs his arm, jumping up and down. "Dad, quickly, come with me!"

He realizes she is serious, and as she jerks his arm even harder, he thinks, "It can't be." He quickly rises to his feet along with several others. They begin to murmur and talk amongst themselves as they hurry to the radio communications lab.

Now this lab, along with some of the others they have built since they have been here, is quite elaborate. They are a little more sophisticated than the ships they landed with. Okay, a lot more sophisticated. They no longer need wheels or arms to crawl or roll along the terrain. They now hover and move along with the orbit of the planet with sophisticated computer technology thanks to Tarvin and Iniria and their floating invention, keeping them at one specific area away from the solar blast of the sun. All of the ships are equipped with this, along with hundreds of yards of metal with dirt on top of them for cultivation, sort of like a planet on top of the planet that moves along the paradise belt safely and securely.

Suslyn's Dad, not knowing what to expect, says, "Hello, is anybody there?"

"Yes, this is Commander Alexander, captain's ship of the Planeterial."

Her dad, after hearing this voice, has a spark of shear joy run through him. He thinks to himself, "Can this be real? The Planeterial? I watched it blow up and be destroyed right here as it entered into the solar blast of the sun."

"Yes, I know all about the Planeterial. It was completely destroyed. We are survivors. How is it even possible that there is a ship?"

"No time for that. I can explain that later. Right now, I need to know how many people are down there and how many people survived."

"Well, there are over one hundred people down here right now. There were seventy five of us with our space shuttles."

"That's all that's left out of over one thousand people?!?" the commander says in disbelief.

"Oh no, no, no, that's not what I'm saying. I'm saying that's all that's on the planet, now," Mr. Traylon says.

"What do you mean? I'm confused. You mean there are other people on other planets?"

"No, a group of scientists got together and created another ship, the Limonium. It is long gone now, gone on to the destination to complete the mission the Planeterial was created to do. We have established life support and other things on this planet and means to survive with minimal threat. Suslyn, my daughter, the one you have been speaking to, is one of the youngest scientists on the planet now. She is over communications and hundreds of other things. Let us know when you reach our atmosphere, and we will shuttle out to meet you."

"I'm afraid it is going to be a while. Our resources on the ship, such as fossil fuels, are about used up. They were used up when I blasted off to get into warp speed, and then the rest of it was used up when I slowed down to turn around to come back. I'm afraid the only thing I can do is hover on the outside of the planet, outside of the atmosphere."

"Don't worry about that. We will send ships out to meet you," Mr. Traylon says.

After the navigation is set to the course and the telemetry is fed to the computer, they warp to the outer atmosphere of the planet, out of harm's way of the solar sun behind the planet, and the commander is met by what he calls colonizers. The captain's ship is left hovering in the outer atmosphere.

Chapter 9
Seven

Soon after arriving, while Woodlynn is analyzing the logs of the destruction of the Planeterial, she realizes that the cosmic blast was the reason the star is so bright. It has been bombarded for thousands and thousands of heaps, and approximately every twenty-five heaps or so, the whole planet is saturated with the bombardment of cosmic rays, the same that destroyed the Planeterial. They roughly have ten heaps left before the whole planet is bombarded again.

Mr. Traylon is a very sophisticated man, along with DD and the team of scientists under them. After hearing this, he is greatly dismazed, especially after they have worked so hard to establish a home. Now, it is going to be destroyed. His daughter, having an exceptional IQ, wishes that she would have been old enough to leave with the Limonium. Her dad is surely glad that she wasn't.

Suslyn and Iniria, although Iniria is a little older, are now best friends. They elaborate and articulate all spot long on scientific stuff, especially about space travel. Iniria's brother, an aviator and genius engineer, is the one that designed their floating city. All Iniria can talk about is what she hears her brother talk about all the time, flying off this planet. They would have left long ago had communications not been disrupted on the planet's surface. Now Iniria spends all spot telling fascinating stories about their adventures surviving on the planet on their own which makes

Suslyn want to travel the cosmos even more. She is none the less jealous in the most righteous way as she listens to Iniria tell her stories.

But now that the planet is in trouble and they only have ten heaps to stay here, they come up with the idea to build a new space station. Commander Alexander comes up with the idea to turn the captain's space ship into a new and improved Planeterial. The computer links up with the other computers on the other ships, and all data resources are updated automatically. There are twenty-five space ships left and more than enough fossil fuel.

Commander Alexander and Woodlynn have had no little romance between them since they met. Being the only two in space, they are very close, all the time loving on each other, hugging on each other. Every time she enters into the room with him, she will kiss him on the lips or on the cheek, sometimes a friendly gesture and sometimes very romantic. The only reason they are not married conventionally is because there was no one to marry them. But now that there are other people, they feel the duty of saying their vows before others is necessary, so they are married.

Now the second generation of people that have been born on the planet are triplets, fourthlets, and fifthlets because of the rich resources upon the planet. Now, the commander and his wife are introduced to it. She is found with child, three boys and four girls. It is a record.

At first, a boy is born. Then another, twins, then another, a third, triplets, three brothers. "Oh my," she thinks to herself. "How am I going to take care of all these kids?"

As the doctor pulls them out, she says, "Oh, here comes another one, a beautiful baby girl, fourthlets. You did say you didn't want to know during the pregnancy. What a beautiful thing to find out, huh? Oh my goodness, here comes another one. Fifthlets!"

Although there is no pain, she can only think, "How can I take care of all these babies? There is so much responsibility I have already." The thought of being a mother overwhelms her even more.

That's when the doctor says, "Here comes another one."

With astonishment, she can't believe her eyes, six babies. She says, "Are you sure that's all, Doctor?"

"Oh, I'm quite sure. That's a record. Five babies is all that has ever been born."

As she is speaking, here comes the head of another one, a baby girl. That's when her momma says, "I will call her Lastley, mainly because she was the last to come out."

Now, the husband of Woodlynn and now father of these seven children stands there in shock. He has been in shock before, but this time, he can't even open his mouth, at least not to say anything. His mouth does drop open the whole time his children are coming into the world one after another. He is finally able to say, "Seven?!? Honey, next time maybe we should let the doctor tell us how many children we are going to have."

"Next time? Well, Alexander, isn't seven children enough for you?" his wife says.

That's when he says the first one will be Theese the Second. He will later be the captain of the new ship. Woodlynn decides to name the second one after her dad, the captain of the Planeterial.

As she thinks about naming her second child, her mind goes back to the last time she saw her dad. That's when she says, "Computer, give me the last entry of my dad."

The computer comes back and says, "Authorize entry. Enabled. Scanning archives."

After the computer scans the archives, it says, "Dr. Woodlynn, a suggestion, if I may?"

"Yes?"

"Well, are you sure you want to see this last entry? It is not the last memory of your father I would recommend you remembering."

"Just show me the archives, please," she tells it.

"Yes, immediately."

After a few moments of watching her dad stand over Glyria's cryo-pod and looking at the expression on his face, she realizes that it is more than just a look. There is passion in his eyes like she hasn't seen in heaps, since she was a little girl.

As soon as she thinks this, she sees her dad take his finger and slide it across the panel. The computer says, "De-cryogenics enabled. De-cryogenics enabled."

After the computer calls him away to navigations, the captain walks away and enters into the navigation room. She hears her dad say, "Quickly, wake my daughter Woodlynn, Commander Alexander, and all the upper level command."

As soon as the computer says, "Communications failure with the captain's shuttle," bright flashes of light light up the whole room. It goes white hot! It instantly burns off the captain's clothes and all the hair off his body. The light goes out. Everything goes dark, and what lighting does come back on shows the captain being sucked through a one foot hole almost instantly.

Woodlynn grabs her eyes, holds her hands tightly on her face, and yells out, "Enough!" Enough! I can't take anymore!"

"What a horrible way to die!" she thinks, crying exhaustively.

As soon as she gets through watching, her husband walks in and sees the horrifying look upon her face. She looks at him sternly. "Did you know? Be honest with me. Did you know?"

He says, "Yes, I knew."

"Do you even know what I'm talking about?"

"If you're talking about your dad's love affair, yes, I know what you're talking about. He talked as if you were awake. I had no idea you were in cryogenics. I just thought you were one of the technicians. I guess that explains why I didn't get to meet you during my shift with the captain, but yes, they were very passionate toward one another. The captain would find some reason to wake Glyria every time his shift came up. I just assumed the captain didn't want me to meet you, but now I realize it is because you were in cryogenics. Matter of fact, I assumed a lot of things."

Just then, Commander Alexander gives the order to the computer, "Computer, Captain Lafi's last log entry."

"Captain Lafi here. Woodlynn, I need to let you know something. Some things have happened while you have been in cryogenics. I was awakened early this time. I have a strange feeling over me, and I can't explain it. But I need you to know my heart. The first thing you need to know is that I loved your mother dearly. I know we've talked, and I know you are against me getting married again. But I met someone before cryogenics, and I didn't have the heart to tell anybody. Well...I'm just going to get to the point. I'm in love, and if we reach the new planet, I will tell you everything you need to know when you wake up. Glyria is her name. She has asked me to wake you up several times. She can't wait to meet you. She is passionate about the things that you are passionate about, and myself. You're gonna like her a lot. Just remember, if anything happens to me, I love you dearly. Captain's log, Out."

After Dr. Woodlynn hears this, she busts out crying and says, "I miss him so much. I've been reluctant to go over the captain's log and the last entries. I guess I just wasn't ready to mourn for his death. But now that I have all these babies, I needed to tie up the loose ends and get on with life. My dad would have wanted it that way."

Her husband looks at her and says, "He certainly would have."

"Did you know her?" she asks.

"Briefly," he answers. "She was a wonderful person. That's all I can tell you about her. She was kind hearted. She would have been a good mother. You would have liked her."

"I already do," Woodlynn says.

After Commander Alexander leaves the room, Woodlynn says, "Computer, Glyria's last entry, please."

The computer comes back and says, "Authorizing archives."

After a rest of searching for a suitable planet to live on, the last moments Glyria spends in haste as she prepares to shuttle off with the captain, commander, and the head scientist. After entering into the shuttle, the second captain sits beside Glyria. The second commander and Dr. Laveman sit across from them.

Just then, she turns to the captain and says, "Captain, I need to tell you something. I was engaged to Captain Lafi to be married. This is the reason I was woke up. After the captain performed his duties, he would wake me up and we would spend a lot of time together."

"How long has this been going on?"

"Since before cryogenics. It started out as a friendly gesture. Right before cryogenics, I told the captain, 'You can wake me if you get lonely.' The next thing I remember is waking up, and then we fell in love."

When Dr. Glyria is about to say another word, the 3D imagery goes white. The computer comes over the intercom and says, "End of Last Entry."

Two heaps later, the space station is well on its way. Extravagant resources have been found upon this planet such as have never been found in any galaxy before. Heavy machinery continually gathers up more resources while shuttle craft blast off to the space station every quarter sector. Computer technologies are so advanced that they are able to create androids and robotic mechanisms that replace the need for human labor, including aviation and piloting the space shuttles. Because the androids do not need resources to operate in space, they are able to work continual segments of time without stopping.

It is now at the end of three heaps since the commander's wife first had children. She is now giving birth to four other children. Now Woodlynn, being a brilliant part of the team and the commander's wife, is pretty much in control of just about everything that the commander is over. Everybody respects her, and when she gives her opinion, everybody listens. Woodlynn estimates the time of the solar blast from the center of the galaxy to be seven heaps, nine leans, and three spots. According to her calculations, they will have to leave in seven heaps to escape the solar system's demolity.

By this time, there are approximately one hundred and seventy-five people, mostly teenagers. One spot during a sector of time, some of the teenagers get off the floating platform which is about ten feet off the surface of the planet. They venture off into a swampy-like area where the plant life is extremely fertile. Vine-like plants grow from the trees down to the ground. It is extremely thick.

After spending a sector of time in the swampy area, they are famished and decide to turn back. After getting back to the levitating city, they climb back up and realize that one of the teenagers is gone. Fear strikes them. One by one, they realize they have to tell the adults. Although the planet moves slowly, it does move, and you don't want to get caught during the move. If they don't find her fast, she will be in harm's way.

There is one animal on the planet called the tatious. Now the tatious is a very tame animal and extremely shy. It has six legs but kind of uses the front legs like arms. It can come up and hug you with the front legs, too. It has paws and a round shaped head with a flat face. It is very loyal to whoever it spends the most time with it, mainly its owner. These tatious animals are great at tracking people, especially if they have the scent of them, like a greyhound canine which has been extinct for many centuries but has been studied in the archives from ancient Earth.

Everybody in the colony is equipped with a tracker, a GPS type of thing, but for some reason, in these deep swampy woods, the signal cannot being picked up. They bring out a particular tatious. They call this tatious, It. The parents of the young teenager bring out some of the clothing that she has once worn. It takes a good whiff, runs about twenty feet, looks back to its owner, waits for the owner to follow, and then runs another good ways. It will not go too far until the owner catches up. Several of the adults follow It through the swampy area.

After about a half a sector, they come upon a great big tree that the children had been climbing over the roots of. Now they are very big roots about three feet off the ground, some two feet, some one foot, but the tatious has no problem climbing or jumping from root to root. After It jumps up on a three feet root, It turns around and looks at its master. When its tail points up in the air, that means it has found something. These roots are three feet in diameter.

There are two of them. In between the two roots, there is a split in the ground. They do not know how deep it goes.

Every suit is equipped with gravitational devices. They can gravitate in any direction. They take off the covers to their light source that is continual around their belts. They point downward toward the ground, and two of the adults float down through the crevice between these two roots. They slowly descend.

When they come to a clearing on a ledge, that's where they see her. Something is pulling her back into the cave-like part. When they levitate over to where she is at, she is hanging on the edge, panting for air. She has held on so long that she finally had to let go, and then her sleeve got caught on a sharp rock. Apparently, she had screamed until she couldn't scream anymore. Now, all she can do is pant. She is in shock.

Craton is one of the adults that spots her first. When the light shines upon her leg, they can see that a plant-like animal has her left leg consumed up to the knee. When he sees this, he takes out a gun-like laser and shoots it halfway down, about a foot away from where her leg should be. There is no light or laser that comes out. You can't see anything come out of the gun, but you can certainly see what it hits. It cuts the plant-like animal right in two. As soon it does, it releases from her leg. Her foot up to her knee is gone. It is horrible! He takes the gun and shoots her leg, cauterizing the wound right below the knee. They sedate her and then grab her and make way to the surface.

When the mom and dad retrieve their daughter, they are in shock when they see that her leg is missing. They take her immediately to the medical bay, put her in a medical pod, and begin reconstruction on the leg. Craton begins to explain to the little girl's dad how he found her and that the plant had dissolved her leg. Had it been too much later, it probably would have consumed her completely.

Running a scan on the little girl, they realize that the chemical that dissolved her leg has run through her blood and contaminated her system. The computer analyzes and quickly begins blood transfusion, but it is too late. It has already reached her main organs. She is dying.

The medical staff begins to analyze the blood further, trying to make an antidote to save the little girl. She isn't coming out of shock. They all articulate on the fact that what is beneath the ground is more deadly than what is above ground. They all come to the conclusion that only robotic and synthetic androids should do any excavation beneath the ground, due to the toxicity of the plants and the diseases that they may carry.

Nigus is a young teenager that has been a scientist from the age of eight heaps old. He is very witty and very smart. After analyzing the blood of the young girl, no one could come up with a cure. Now, Nigus takes up where the other scientists left off and begins to analyze her blood on his own. He notices that the virus when it attaches itself to the blood cells will replicate on the red blood cells, but on the white blood cells, it will grow.

When Nigus tries to grab the glass-like slide that the girl's blood is on that he is looking at through a microscope, it cuts the side of his finger. His blood is A negative while the little girl's blood type is AB positive. His blood gets onto her blood. He thinks to himself, "Oh no! I've contaminated the blood. Now, I won't be able to examine it further."

But when he looks back through the microscope again, he notices something peculiar. The white blood cells from the A negative blood are not killing the white blood cells of the AB positive blood. Instead, they are attaching themselves to the other blood cells. When this happens, the virus dies, turning black, which the liver will be able to filter out like all other contamination. It is converting the blood to O blood type.

Nigus rushes to share this information with the head scientist over the lab, and then the head scientist tells the parents of the young girl. He elaborates with them, saying that a transfusion like this will kill the girl because it is the wrong blood type. The parents are all for it, but the head scientist is against it.

After hearing them debate for several moments, Nigus takes it upon himself to extract some of his own blood. He takes the syringe and places it in the girl's arm, injecting it without their permission.

After a few moments of watching her, she begins to pant real heavy and real fast. Sweat begins pouring out of her pores. As she wakes up in terror, she screams at the top of her lungs and then passes out from the pain. He thinks to himself, "Oh my gosh! What have I done!"

Her breathing goes from a fast deep breathing to a slow deep breathing and then to normal. When the parents and lab technicians hear her scream, they come running in to see what has happened. The young teenager, Nigus, stands there as they look at her. They look at him meanly, knowing what he has done.

"She was dying anyway," he tells them. "Something had to be done."

That's when she opens her eyes and says, "It hurts. It's so painful."

But after the pain dies down and she regains full consciousness, she says, "I'm starting to feel better now."

The head scientist over the medical bay then takes a sample of her blood and places it into the computer for analyzation. The virus is dead. Her blood is now O type blood. The computer articulates, explaining that this is likely the reason why it was so painful. All of her organs had to take the new type of blood, and the conversion was extremely exhausting and painful.

After restoration to her organs is finished, her color comes back, and she feels a whole lot better. That's when shock runs through her body as she looks upon her leg that isn't there, a prosthetic. The pod rebuilt her leg, but she knows it isn't hers. She begins to weep.

The young teenage boy takes her by the hand and shakes his head side to side, saying, "You are lucky to be alive at all."

She looks at him, saying, "I know." She speaks very quietly, still saddened by the loss of her leg.

Right away, the head technician gives the order to an android to go back to the location where the young girl was found. The android is called 503. After 503 has been gone for a half a sector, it returns with part of the plant in a large flask with a lid on it.

"What do you plan to do with this? May I ask?" 503 asks.

"Well, this completely changed the blood type of a person without killing them. Not only did it convert it, but after the introduction of a different blood type, it completely cleansed it," he explains. "So, it is both a virus and, with another type of blood added to it, an antidote. I want to invent a formula using this plant so that when someone gets a blood disease, we can introduce this into the blood, add another blood type, and completely alter the blood, cleansing it."

"Extravagant idea," 503 replies. "I am surprised I did not think of that myself."

Now many new species of plant life like this one have been found on the surface of this planet. Thousands of other formulas have been introduced over the past twelve heaps. Not to mention the animal life, which is also very peculiar. One animal in particular is related to a flounder in the oceans of Earth. It crawls along the ground. Nobody would have ever known that it existed until they were building the levitating city.

They had a ladder going up to the levitated part of the city, and every so often, they had to move the ladder. On this particular spot of time, the ladder was stuck up on top of this particular animal. It was camoflauged just like the ground it was on until that ladder was stuck right on top of it. It was about three feet in diameter. It let out a high penetrating hiss, "Ssssss."

It hurt everybody's ears and began to squabble, trying to get away out from under the ladder. It could not. Although it was plenty strong enough to get out from underneath the ladder, it did not. It just stayed there, wobbling up and down. Finally, the engineer that was working on the platform grabbed the ladder off the top of it. It acted as if it was severely wounded. After close examination of the animal, they realized that it was just terrified.

Now, shortly after Commander Alexander had children and moved onto the floating city, they are working on attaching some more of their ships to the floating city. When Commander Alexander exits the last ship, he smells a wonderful smell. It is intoxicating! He thinks to himself, "I haven't smelled that in a long time."

Finally, he can't stand it any longer. "Where is that smell coming from?" he asks.

That's when one of the aviator engineers speaks up and says, "My little sister is cooking up some coffee. Would you like some?"

"Would I ever?!?"

"You like coffee, do you?" the aviator asks.

"Yeah, what's your name?"

"Oh, I'm Tarvin. I'm an aviator engineer," he answers.

As Tarvin's little sister pours them both a cup of coffee, the commander says, "I don't mind saying this. You're my new best friend now."

Tarvin says, "Well, I don't mind that a bit, but I've got a feeling I'm going to be an even better friend after I tell you what I'm fixing to tell you. You see out that window?"

"Yes," the commander answers.

"You see that great big bush?"

"Yes, the one with the little red berries?"

"Yes," Tarvin says with a smile. "You know what those little red berries are? Inside those red berries is coffee. It yields a hundred pounds a lean. Those big ol' sacks you're sitting on. That's coffee."

"There must be a thousand pounds here!" the commander exclaims.

"More," Tarvin tells him. "By the time we get this space station built, we will probably have enough to secure us with coffee indefinitely, especially if we take this little bush."

"And you only have one of those that puts out all this coffee?"

"Well, we only had one seed left, and we didn't know exactly what it was when we found it. Apparently, everybody loved coffee and used it up really quick. But I took this seed and put it out there. I didn't even bury it. Several sectors went by, and I got to looking. It was almost four feet high. Now it is seven feet high, and it won't get any bigger. But every time you pick those little berries off, two or three gather in the same spot, and now every limb is soaked with the berries. There's hardly any room for anymore to get on it. The leaves have to squeeze out between the berries so the leaves can get their photosynthesis. You bust the seed out of the berry, dry it out, cook it up, and its coffee."

Tarvin then says, "Commander, I never got a chance to meet you, but I did get a chance to meet the captain before cryogenics. It has certainly been a pleasure to meet you now. I heard you married the captain's daughter."

That's when the commander says, wide-eyed and awake, "Well, who is this beautiful young lady that makes such a wonderful cup of coffee?"

She smiles and says, "My name is Iniria."

Tarvin then speaks up and says, "Yes, she is kind of shy. I think it is because her brain is working full load constantly, so it completely puts her in another world most of the time than what me and you live in," Tarvin teases her.

Iniria says, "Not all the time. I did come back to fix your coffee, as I usually do."

Tarvin smiles and says, "And a good cup at that," as he tilts his cup toward her.

The commander does the same. Not realizing that this cup of coffee is stronger than what he was used to, he begins to speak really fast and get excited as he asks, "Now, what do I have to do to get one of these bags I'm sitting on?"

"One? Take two or three. I've got so much I don't know where to store it at. That's why you're sitting on one right now as a chair."

"Yeah, I can see how I would want coffee instead of a chair. And I know the perfect place to store it all. Right on my ship. I've got a big ol' bay that will hold as much as you want to put on there, and any other valuables you want to put in there," the commander tells him. He smiles and adds, "You know, for safekeeping and all."

Tarvin smiles, too, as he says, "There is another ancient thing that you may not be aware of, Commander. Try some of this in your coffee. You see those round things at the bottom of that coffee bush?"

"Yeah, the vines that grow, the big green things about one foot in diameter?"

"Well, we thought that was just a root at first until one spot when we busted the hard shell on the outside. When we did, the stuff just oozed out. Now, if you get that stuff on you, it's quite sticky, so we brought it in to the computer and had it analyzed. The computer said it was an ancient syrup called honeydew. After further research, I went back even farther and found out these little insects made it, and then I found out that it wasn't honeydew at all. It was called honey. The little insects would put it in some kind of waxy substance, but this particular plant produces the exact same process without the insect."

"What exactly is an insect?" the commander asks.

"Not really sure. I didn't research that part out. I was just more concerned about this sweet stuff that's quite mess. But some fell in my coffee one morning, and when I tasted it, it tasted really incredible."

The commander says, "I agree. I'm gonna need some of this honey, too."

"Sure, take all you want," Tarvin tells him. "It's a never ending supply. They grow wild everywhere."

Now, everybody on the platform has cultivated some type of fruit or another, usually their favorite. They are constantly trading out. Soon, everybody has coffee. Everybody has honey. Everybody has melons of all kinds, and it isn't long until the commander has filled up the bay with all kinds of little treats.

But the most special thing is a plant called cowtin. Now this plant grows limbs on it about six inches thick. It grows about six feet long, and when you cut into it, it has a bone in the middle of it. It is like flesh. If you take this meat and put it over a fire, it is the most delicious stuff. That, with onion, potato, and a good cup of coffee with honey...well, nothing more needs to be said. Now, meat is a precious commodity, and no one has had real meat for thousands of heaps. The livestock has been so genetically altered that even the meat tastes like water, if it has any taste at all. But this plant here has an unbelievable flavor.

The biggest consumers of the coffee are the jumpers, which the commander calls adrenaline addicts. After the commander and Tarvin consume a cup of coffee early one spot, Mrs. Baldren walks up and says, "Do you have an extra cup?"

Tarvin says, "Sure."

She introduces herself to the commander, and Tarvin introduces him to her. Mrs. Baldren says, "I'm surprised my husband hasn't already tried to get you to jump off the canyons. Anyway, it's nice meeting you, Commander," she says as she walks off with her cup of coffee.

Tarvin then says, "The jumpers are quite high strung. I think I might have a little bit to do with that, with my coffee."

The commander says, "Yeah, the computer says it's the stuff in the coffee called caffeine."

Tarvin says, "Yeah, it seems harmless enough."

That's when Iniria says, "Yeah, some people shouldn't have coffee."

Tarvin looks at Iniria with a hush hush look. She says, "Well, it's true. They're quite rude and a little reckless if you ask me."

That's when Dr. Baldren walks up and says, "Oh, you're talking about me, are you?"

Iniria turns and walks away as she goes to get another cup of coffee, knowing exactly what he has come for.

Baldren turns to the commander and says, "My wife says she just met you. My name is Baldren. I'm the head over the jumpers, so to speak. Would you like to join us for this spot?"

The commander raises his eyebrows and says, "You mean, do I

want to jump off a cliff into a canyon for no reason and fall for miles and maybe even fall to my sudden death? Risk my life?"

"No better way to start your spot, Commander," Baldren says.

Tarvin says, "I can think of a few better ways."

Baldren looks at him and says, "Yeah, Tarvin. We already know how scared you are."

"It's not the fall I'm afraid of. It's that sudden stop," Tarvin tells him.

Baldren snickers as he asks, "What about you, Commander? Are you going to back out, too?"

After thinking of a few choice words and being a little bit jittery from the cups of coffee he has had, the commander says, "There's a lot of work to be done. You know, instead of spending all spot jumping off into a canyon, maybe you could lend a helping hand."

"Not a chance, Commander. These canyons come around one season out of the heap," Baldren says as he walks away. "Besides that, leaving this place is your thing. I'm not so sure we need to leave at all."

That's when Iniria walks out the door and says, "See what I mean?" as she looks at Tarvin. The commander doesn't say anything.

As the leans and then heaps go by, Commander Alexander and Tarvin become very close friends, and they all soon realize how smart Iniria really is. When Woodlynn meets her, they hit it off right off the bat, so to speak. When they start speaking their scientific terminology, it is like another language. Nobody understands a word they say. Iniria even wrote a math language that Woodlynn is able to pick up almost immediately. Then, she shares some of the languages she has written. When they start talking about molecular structures, warp factors, and bending time, the commander stands astonished, amazed at how smart his wife really is. Most of the time, he does not know what she is talking about even though he is an extreme genius himself.

Tarvin, on the other hand, understands one thing about his sister. She is smart, and he can't touch it. Iniria realizes one thing about her brother. He can create or fix anything. But these two together, they can't be touched. They are inseparable. And now they are building a space station.

Chapter 10
Time To Leave

After four heaps into the build of the new space station, a problem is brought to the engineers' attention. One of the metals found on the surface which is needed for the main structures of the frame of the ship, after being in a no atmosphere climate such as space, has begun to deteriorate. It is the strongest and most valuable material on the planet, but now it is turning into powder.

The main architect of the ship who is head over the engineers has to think fast. That's when Commander Alexander, after getting news of the deterioration, commands, "Quick, look up the doc files on what they did to the Limonium to fix this. At this deterioration rate, in a couple of spots of time, we will not have any ship at all."

The computer quickly uploads the information. There is a yellow algae in the northern hemisphere that grows up on the mountain peaks after the cold section. It looks almost like snow on the peaks except it is yellow. If you take this algae and genetically mix it with the substance in the sand pits, then genetically mix it into the metal, it creates an internal atmosphere for the metal itself which totally makes it indestructible. This most crucial thing was overlooked during the process of building. The commander goes to the head engineer and asks why this was overlooked.

The head engineer says it wasn't overlooked. "Third in command took care of that," he says.

That's when the third in command comes up, and they ask him

what happened. He says, "We made a batch. It was all mixed in with the metal. Everything was done right as far as I know. It should not be deteriorating."

The head engineer then asks for a sample of the batch. After the computer analyzes it, it says, "The batch is correct, but there seems to be a small added ingredient of .001 percent of an unknown material."

The head lab scientist begins to analyze the origin of the unknown material. Apparently, while the batch was set up on the ground, some airborne debris got in it that it took away atmosphere, contaminating the whole batch. They have to work fast. They fly ships over to the other side of the planet and begin to gather up the algae while land rovers are filled up with the other material, Sanulite. Mixed together, they called it the Sanulite compound, at least that's the name the Limonium crew gave it.

Now, panels have to be removed to get to the inner structure of the ship. The compound is then applied. This kills the anti-atmosphere contamination and saves what metal is there. The metal that was already deteriorated has to be replaced along with the other metal panels that it has touched. It is a long, hard process. After de-structuring and adding the new compound, the structure is added back, and the construction is well on the way. It puts them almost a heap behind.

The Limonium was built by almost one thousand people. They have to build another space station with a only a tenth of that many people in less time with less scientists. More androids are made on a daily basis. At the end of four heaps, almost a thousand androids are working around the spot. By the end of the fifth heap, there are almost fifteen hundred androids.

During the creation of the space station, the heavy metals will smash the androids if they get in a pinch point which totally destroys their processing units. They are basically good for nothing after that. Due to the massive amounts of heavy metals that are being moved, damage is done on just about every spot, if they aren't completely destroyed. Two out of five androids after thirty spots of time go completely out. They get heavily damaged and cease to work.

Now, Tarvin, being an aviator engineer, realizes the value of these androids and the time it takes to create them. It takes thirty scientists to create one in thirty spots of time, but now the androids are creating the other androids in about fifteen spots of time. He comes up with an idea.

The androids have ejector suits which make them able to fly in space which leaves them using their hands to fly with instead of being able to handle what they are doing. He comes up with a suit that is integrated into their processors that will automatically do the flying while they are able to work, handle the heavy metals, and get themselves out of pinch points in a hurry.

It works great. Instead of two being created every thirty spots and two getting destroyed every thirty spots, two are now created every fifteen to thirty spots, and one will get destroyed every half a heap or so. After fifteen hundred more androids are made, another heap and a half has gone by. They are now ahead of schedule instead of behind.

Now Commander Alexander has carried the title commander the whole time, but being that he is now captain of a star ship, he decides that he needs a first officer. Now Tarvin, being his best friend, is naturally nominated by him, but the computer analyzes the statistics and says that Tarvin is not the best analytically but would be politically. Although Tarvin is not one of the top geniuses, his analytical skills and survival skills are put into the calculation, and after long debate, the choice comes between the captain's wife, who is the head of the science team, and Tarvin, who was already head of aviation in the prior ship.

The decision is left up to the captain, and after debating with his wife three quarters through a spot, he realizes she does not want to give up her position over the science department. The captain says, "Well, it's settled, then. Commander Tarvin will be sworn in at the same time I am sworn in as captain."

That's when he stops and says to his wife, "Oh, by the way, you may not be commander, but I'm making you third in command. That still leaves you head over the scientists."

It is a big deal being sworn in. Everybody is excited. It is very political. That is when the name of the space station is given. After long debate, they do not see any reason to change the names on all the space ships. So, the previous name is continued, along with an honor to the late Captain Lafi. The name is written on the side of the ship. "The Planeterial" with "Lafi 3523," written underneath in small capital letters.

After the captain is sworn in, the commander is next in line, and he is sworn in, too. The heads of each department come up and shake Commander Tarvin and Captain Alexander's hands.

That's when Tarvin's little sister looks up at him and says, "You've come quite a long way, haven't you? Your time was due, I think."

"Yeah, but commander over a space station?" he says.

"I would say long overdue," she says. "My big brother, Commander."

Now, this space station is twice the size of the Planeterial, and getting the atmosphere and oxygen levels correct is a big deal. That's when they use the big balloon-like plants they have found by the thousands. These balloon-like plants are all over the planet this heap, very plentiful. Each one is blown up with oxygen which can be filled up in a hundred yard diameter and then taken to the space station where generator pumps suck the oxygen out of the balloons into the space station, giving it an oxygen rich environment.

After the space station is filled, the balloon-like plants are used as oxygen tanks along with fluid tanks. They are more than suitable for the tasks they perform, each different from the other one. The ship has corridors filled with these balloon-like tanks. Even if they bust, the corridors will hold the liquid-like oxygen, so nothing is lost in space if one of them busts. Each corridor has its own liquid-like substance. Oxygen for one. Helium for another one. Rocket fuel in another one. These are like giant bladders inside of the corridors.

Now the laser guidance system is introduced. It is a very simple navigation system, unlike any others before its time. Its needle pin-like laser is simply pointed to its direction, and its laser-like engines are magnetically pulled to the point of origin. There are fifty laser pointers around the ship. It looks rather cool when in operation. Fifty pin-like lasers shoot into the dark of space, and then the warp drive is introduced. It starts off slow at first, but after a few moments, it will completely disappear before your eyes.

This phenomenal research is introduced by Tarvin's sister, Iniria, and her dearest friend, Suslyn, along with Dr. Woodlynn's help. These three work around the spot, inventing some of the most advanced technologies, even more advanced than the technology of the Limonium or its predecessor, and those two were ahead of their time.

There is no need for lights on the ship. Inside and out is coated with a paint-like substance that gives off three thousands lumens per inch around the spot in every part of the ship which makes it quite bright throughout the ship, inside and out. It is a beautiful glowing white ship in space when it is finished.

The ship has twenty-four navigation systems and over thirty power sources, six of which can engage warp drive to phenomenal speeds. The communications systems have two backups for each backup up to twenty-five backups, each one more elaborate than the next. They are continually updated on the spot every spot of time.

All the individual space ships are immaculate size. If need be, they can support fifty people easily. That's a cramped situation. They can support five people for twenty heaps, ten at ten heaps, twenty people for five heaps, and indefinitely if food is cultivated for a maximum number of twenty people. This is just the on board resources.

There are several cultivating rooms on each ship. There is compressed genetic soil compressed to a portion the size of a small cup that will inflate into the equivalent of a one hundred pound bag of soil, and it only weighs a half an ounce. The heaviest things on these ships are those that occupy them. Each ship is equipped with enough life support to run the ship indefinitely, theoretically. The fewer the people, the more comfortable they will be as far as food and other lodgings.

Now, throughout the station, each room has its own computer system. There is a main system on board on one end of the ship and a secondary main computer on the other end of the ship. If one end blows up, the other end of the ship can still maintain for an indefinite time.

Underneath the captain's quarters on one end, there are about sixteen different types of rocket engines, laser engines, solar powered engines, nuclear powered engines, and two or three fusion powered engines. On the other end is the same thing. This station can go just as fast one way as it can the other. There is not a tail end. The cockpit that is over these engines controls the engines on the opposite side and vice versa. If something happens internally to one end, there are exploding bulk locks on every section of the ship, so if it has to, it can blow totally in half and still be able to be navigated from the other end or from the same end if need be.

There are six different types of force fields, mainly the fifty-five that were on the original Planeterial combined into six with some very special additions. These can almost take a gamma blast directly head on for a few seconds. After that, nothing can withstand a gamma blast. Underneath the glowing paint, there are several different layers of different types of metal, each one harder as it goes deeper. The outside shell of each ship and the station is two feet thick. It has over sixty layers of different metals within these two feet, each one able to withstand different things: radiation, penetration, radio waves, microwaves, just about anything imaginable on and off the periodic table.

The glass in the front of the ship is littonite, and it is three feet thick. If something hits that, it will come closer to busting the whole block out in one piece than it will cracking the littonite. The windows throughout the ship when the blast shields are up are about one inch thick. They don't need to be any thicker, being that the blast shields are almost two and a half feet thick.

Now the space station itself has twenty-five different bulkheads and thirty-five bays which hold nothing but fuels, oxygen, and other gasses, along with a CO_2 converter which will take carbon dioxide, along with any type of airborne contamination, any unbreathable gasses or poisons, out of the air and turn it back into oxygen. There is no need for filters because of this extravagant process. Each space suit is equipped with the same type of filtration. The process is called the Nigus filter, named after its inventor.

Radioactive materials are carried in a special port that spins around the back side of the ship like a halo which surfaces a mile off the hull of the space station. It angles off the back with four blades attaching it to the ship. It has a second halo that spins around that is half the size of that one. It carries some of the stored foods which have been cryolized and dehydrated. That also includes the breeding of any kind of animal and livestock that they may eat, which at this point is very little.

The overall space station is equipped with CG 100 blaster cannons. The CG stands for cosmic gun. The 100 means it is one hundred inches diameter, which makes it big enough for a man to walk all the way upright from one end to the other. All the ship's radiation and contamination are gathered up and used in these cannons to make their cosmic blast. These guns are massive. These are located all over the space station. It can also be a battle station if it has to be. These are mainly for secondary precautions in case the force fields let some of the debris through.

Now with the blast doors down, the back of the windows become gigantic screens. The windows themselves magnify everything on the outside of the ship by one thousand times. The super techno cameras on the outside of each window pane reflect the image to the back part of the littonite on the inside of the ship throughout the whole ship. Whether the blast shields are up or down, it doesn't matter. You still see the same thing.

After this technology is introduced, one of the scientists asks, "Why have windows at all?"

The captain and the crew articulate on the matter and say, "Just in case the power fails."

Tanika, the ship's log officer, joins the conversation and says, "You know, there is just something about being able to do certain things on your own without electronics. And one of them is to be able to see."

Now the rooms are extremely bright at three thousand lumens per inch. The ceiling of every room has a drop ceiling with a one inch light screen. This screen can darken or lighten. It is four inches off the ceiling, and it also is four inches off the wall. There is also a raised floor that does the same thing. This is in every room.

There are no monitors throughout the ship except for the windows. The screens also put out 3D imagery which is most life-like. You either speak it or motion your hand toward the 3D image to move it, manipulate it, or vice versa. It is extremely sophisticated even to the minor details.

Everything is sophisticated, even the lavaratory where the showers are. Exact measurements of water are used for sanitation, sterilization, and other hygiene mechanisms, like laser flash hair removal. You can just hold your head up at a certain angle, and the computer flashes a laser upon your face or wherever you want the hair burnt off and removes the hair without affecting the skin. Haircuts are the same. The hair is then processed into clothing. Deterioration of clothing is very rare, but rips and tears are not. Everything on board is reprocessed or renewed in one fashion or another.

Now, cryogenics are sophisticated way beyond the means of the first Planeterial pods or even the Limonium's space gel. There is now no need for pods at all. The specially designed space suits are more like armored tanks. As soon as you go into the space suit, cryogenics start on thirty percent of your body. If you are sitting and resting, full cryogenics kick in.

The cryogenics stage kicks out when a certain thing is needed. Per say, if you are a pilot, and the ship does not need a pilot at the time and you want to sleep, you can sleep indefinitely in your suit until you are needed. When the cryogenics state is over with, you are fully awake, no slumbering, no throwing up the green stuff.

The new found plants on the surface are liquified and turned into a gas that is merged with the suit along with moisture rejuvenation and waste recycling within the suit. Solids are disposed of based on the individual's hygiene. The sleep is not needed during the process of cryogenics. You can hibernate for a hundred heaps and still be able to process information as it is fed to you during the monitorization of the computer.

There are many special things on board to make one want to stay awake, but the biggest thing that makes one want to stay awake is the fear of not waking up. But after a while, everyone is at ease. If the cryogenics suits go bad, you can simply think, and it will automatically bring you out of cryogenics so you can replace the part of the suit that is bad and go back into cryogenics. So far, no one has had this problem in testing.

There is a sleep stage that happens every spot of time for your brain to rejuvenate. This gives them the REM that their brains need. But after long investigation and technological finds, they realize that only fifteen moments of REM is actually needed per spot for your brain. Most people choose to take a sector. The most special thing about the suits, which are micro-subatomic powered, is that you can fly around in space while you are in them. At full power, the take off of the suits is 1G. One can go one hundred miles in a quarter sector.

Everyone has individual personal prompts which are mini mega computers. Each one has both a flat screen and a visual 3D virtual reality which stems from one inch by two inch and is worn on the wrist of their suits. Or, there is a five by seven micro-thin pad which rolls up and looks sort of like a stylus that can go in a pocket specially designed for it on the outside arm of the suit.

Everyone has two or three of these. Once it is opened up, it instantly knows the location and mapping of the area. It is the most sophisticated part of the suit and personal mechanism and the most valued on board.

Now, each room is equipped with virtual reality, and you can do virtual activities around the spot. Anything from archery, martial arts, ancient gunnery, ancient laser tag, and safari and wood-like adventures, that includes mountain climbing, sky diving, and all the things found in the ancient logs from Earth. Networking together is not recommended more than a few spots a lean each heap. Most agree that they will articulate the tenth and the twentieth spot of each lean for the most part. This is to ensure that everybody knows everybody, at least in an acquantative manner. This makes it easier to keep up with one another, and it also ensures the awareness of the crew mates. Too much entertainment can become a distraction.

The only ones that will have direct communication with the captain are those that are the head of each department along with those on the command post. Those directly under the heads will be able to communicate with the heads. Those under them can communicate with them, and so on. The chain of command is never to be broken. You have to go to the head of your department. To speak to the captain, he will have to get a hold of you after it goes through the chain of command if he deems it important enough. Each head will have ten people under them. The captain will have twenty. There are ten people in the command post, ten heads of each department, ten people under each one of those heads, and so on.

As the children reach a pre-determined age, they will be assigned to a department under a head. There will never be more than ten people under a head. The captain is the head of everybody.

Those on the command post are the head of everybody else other than the captain. The heads of each department are the head of everybody under them, and etc.

This way, there are constant overseers in every little thing everyone does. With several hundred androids on board and a main computer for every room, you can't make a mistake. Whether you are in the scientific department or the maintenance department, whether you were captain of the ship or any other position, there is no minor job. Every job is just as important as the next. There is no discrimination whatsoever on board the ship. Age is irrelevant. It doesn't matter if you are five heaps old or twenty-five heaps old, your IQ and doctorates will determine your position.

Now, all the resources have been gathered into the ship. The planet's resources and artifacts are plentiful, but everyone can't take everything they have found. There are elaborate jewels, gold, platinum, and metals even more rare than rhodium, palladium, and iridium, and several other precious metals.

The captain gives the order to evacuate the planet. Some are happy, and some are bawling their eyes out. Some are joyful, and some are sorrowful. But for the most part, everyone is overwhelmed.

The ships take off one by one, and as they dock in their bays, their ships become part of the space station which will be their primary lodging. Their secondary lodging will be on the space station. Everyone on board that does not have a family is paired up with a partner of their choice out of the selected few that the computer chooses from their department. There are two partners on each ship, which is about four people. Every family has a ship of their own. The commander still holds the record for the most kids born at one time, but the record for having the most kids under ten is twenty-seven kids. Any family that has a family of fifteen or more has two ships that are combined together.

The kids have not been counted in the numbering of the ship's crew which started out at a little under two hundred, but with the children and babies, it is closer to four hundred population. This keeps the androids quite busy, which gives the parents leeway to do their job without distractions. Parenting is everybody's job, especially the computer's.

Schooling is a constant update from one spot to another. Everybody is taught in an orderly fashion. Once a person is in their space suit, the inside of the helmet becomes a virtual reality screen, so they are constantly taught around the spot. During cryogenics, special contact lenses are stuck in each person's eyes, and special listening devices are inside their helmets. Once in cryogenics, everybody is continually updated with what is going on in the ship including its whereabouts and the major decisions that are made. After the incident fifteen heaps ago, nobody wants to wake up with a surprise like that again, the horrifying news of dying or not knowing if you are going to live the next moment or not.

The last ship leaves the planet, at least that's what the captain thinks. He has sent back radio communications to see if any frequency is open. He has sent probes down to the planet and circled the belt around the spot to look for survivors. After three rests of searching for survivors, the probes returned back to the space station. It is time.

Chapter 11
What Can Go Wrong Will Go Wrong

The captain gives the order for the impulse engines to start taking them out of the solar system, and slowly, they drift as they plot the course. Trajectory is plotted, along with the telemetry, and other necessary calculations are calculated in. The captain gives orders for full impulse.

Now, warp drive is not like a conventional warp drive. You have to go impulse to full impulse and then engage warp speed. As warp speed starts, you can watch the ship leave as it gets faster and faster. There are ten clicks to warp. The first click is half light. Full light is light speed. To get to half light takes almost a half a lean. Once to full light, the second click kicks in. This is where you actually warp from one place to another. You can go as far as from one galaxy to the next. Each click warps you that much farther into the future. It takes about five heaps to get to the full ten clicks.

If it is a million light heaps away, you can get there in ten heaps. Now, coming out of warp, you have to click down the same way you went up into warp or the g-force will kill you, so the destination for a million heaps away would take five heaps up and five heaps down, a half a heap for each click. There are other warp drives that have been developed like those used on the Limonium, but due to the documentation and the communication with the computer, the scientists think that this type of warp is more appropriate and less dangerous than blasting your pathway through space.

After the command is given to go into the third click, which is twice light speed, Suslyn's voice comes over the communications com, "Captain Alexander, come quick!"

Now for Que and Serena, trying to establish communication with others has been useless. Until one spot, when they get a message back after sending a message asking if anybody is on the frequency. It is the Planeterial Lafi 3523, leaving the solar system.

"Hello, is anybody there?" Suslyn repeats. She is scanning through many frequencies on the way out of the galaxy.

She hears a voice say it back, "Hello, is anybody there?"

Once again, the first thing she thinks is that someone is tricking her because it is the old frequency of the first space shuttles that landed on the planet. She says, "Okay, the joke's on me. Who is this?"

That's when Serena says, "This is Serena. I was a scientist on the Planeterial. We are stranded on the planet we think they call the paradise belt planet."

"Are you kidding me?!?" Suslyn says.

"Please help us if you can. There are over twety of us on the planet."

Suslyn, now realizing this is not a joke, replies, "This is the Planeterial, the new space station. How is radio communication from this frequency able to get this far off the planet?"

"I don't know," Serena answers. "But there are quakes and tremors all over and lightning blasts high up in the skies in the atmosphere like we have never seen before."

"I am sorry to give you the bad news, but solar blasts, such as those that destroyed the first Planeterial space station, are about to hit the paradise belt planet again. It happens every twenty heaps or so," Suslyn tells her.

"But, we have been here more than twenty heaps," Serena says.

"Yes, for some reason, the solar blasts were analyzed the wrong way and miscalculations were ingested by the computer. It just so happens it is every twenty-six heaps or so, but nevertheless, it is about to happen. What side of the planet are you on right now?"

"We are on the northern hemisphere on the right side," Serena tells her.

By this time, Suslyn has communicated with the captain, and he gets on the frequency. He is having a hard time believing that they have left others stranded on the planet. "There is a good possibility that ya'll might survive the solar blasts, but I am afraid we cannot come back for you," he tells them.

"What do you mean you can't come back for us? You mean you're not on the planet?"

"No, we were on the planet for heaps building a space station in the outer atmosphere. We have been traveling to the outside of the galaxy, waiting for warp speed for the last heap. We are now on the edge of the Y2DB galaxy, far from the solar system you are in. We have been waiting for the solar blasts to start before we hit warp, which could be any spot of time now," the captain explains.

When Serena hears this, she is struck to the heart. She tells her husband the news. When Que hears this, he thinks to himself. "We can survive this with the soil that will not be penetrated by the heat of the blasts." He knows they can survive, but can the planet? Will there be a surface to come back to?

That's when he gets on the communications and asks why they can't come back.

"You don't understand," the captain says. "We can't take the chance of being solar blasted by the massive blasts from the inner

172

core of this galaxy. There are too many people on board."

After Que and Serena explain what happened to them, how they sunk into the pits and lived there for eight heaps and the rest of their tragic story, the captain articulates further on how they built a space station and thought they had retrieved everybody from the surface of the planet.

He also tells them about the Limonium. "A lot has happened while you were underground," he says. "We are going to send you data of the precious resources that we have located and schematics of everything we have done. If you survive, the coordinates and navigation of where we are going will be included. I am sending you the information now."

As the ship's computer downloads the data, the captain keeps articulating on the fact that they cannot come back because there are too many people on board whose lives the survival of mankind is depending on. "If you make it, I hope to see you in the future," he tells them.

Now, Cadum, upon hearing this news, is struck to the bone with anger. He pounds his fists into the palm of his other hand. "This is not fair," he thinks to himself. "All this time, we strove to get to the surface and then to survive." He has so hoped to meet other people besides his brothers and sisters.

Teah, upon hearing the news, goes up onto high ground, where she has often visited, a place with a very, very beautiful offset. No one has ever visited there but her. Cadum, watching her walk away, follows her at a distance. He sees her sit down on one of the stumps that was burnt off during the prior rotation of the planet, put her hands on her face, and bust out crying.

She says to herself, "I am never going to see my friends again. There is no one but me in this big ol' planet."

Cadum, never having the courage before, is now filled with

zeal, knowing he has nothing to lose anyway. He goes to Teah, picks her up off where she is sitting, puts his arms around her, and kisses her very, very romantically.

Her eyes are open at first as she is held there in shock of what Cadum has just done, but after the moment passes and he keeps his lips pressed firmly against hers, she can't keep her eyes open any longer. She grunts once, "Hmmm." Then she grunts again as she closes her eyes again. As she grunts the third time, she puts her arms around him.

She has never felt this before. She grunts one more time, this time it is longer than all three of the others. The feelings she has never had before are compiled all into one moment. She doesn't know what she is feeling, but it feels better than anything she has ever experienced. Then, she realizes that she is terribly in love as she opens her eyes slowly and looks into his. Their moments of passion cannot be expressed with words. The fear of dying, the tragedy that is about them, can't touch the way they feel. After a sector, they return to their home and safe haven.

When they return back, holding hands, giggling, smiling, and admiring one another, Serena, seeing her son so happy as she has never seen before, knows what has happened but asks anyway. "Now what's going on with you two?"

His dad turns around and says as if he doesn't know, "Yes, what are you two so happy about?"

That's when Fleece turns around, and for the first time ever, jealousy hits him because he has never been in love before, mainly because he couldn't crunch the numbers of it. But knowing Teah the way he does and realizing that she is able to crunch the numbers makes him somewhat jealous, mainly because it makes her appear smarter than himself in the fact that she has found love against all odds.

After Cadum and Teah are married, they come up with the idea, after going through the schematics and charts of the first two star ships that were built, that since they have a ship that will reach the outer plummets of the solar system, that they will build their own station. Knowing that the solar system as they know it is about to be plummeted with plasmatic gamma rays, whether they are going to live or die, they are planning for the future.

They get to work. The first thing they do is build a two feet gorge around the ship. Then, they build a platform that will encase the entire ship like a box. Then, they build a four feet box on the outside of it, leaving a hole in the top. They pour the material they had sunk down into from the start, which they now call plesacon, in through the hole. They use layers of metal on the outer layers that can withstand extreme heat. Using technology from the new Planeterial's data files, they make laser cutters for the outermost shell using the strongest of the metals. They also do this to every living quarters. Beneath each moat, they dig a ten feet hole in diameter going beneath it to get under the box to get to the ship and the homes.

They build one large facility for everybody to gather into and live in during the time of the solar blasts. It is underground. The plesacon is poured on top of it approximately ten feet deep. This facility is very elaborate. They are able to build all kinds of drilling facilities, machinery, and find many rare metals because of the data they were sent. By this time, several androids have been developed from the schematics in the data transfer as well as other computer systems. They gather as many resources as they can and store them in the underground facility. Heat resistant metals are also placed on top of it all, above ground. They do not stop working around the spot.

They say their goodbyes as the new Planeterial station warps

175

away from their galaxy. Last plans and last moment data is sent. Now, it is time to go underground.

Quelana is the oldest girl that Serena gave birth to during her second pregnancy. She was the first girl. She is now going on twenty heaps of age. She gathers with her family in the main quarters of the facility as they wait for the solar blasts to go through the galaxy. Some fear for their lives. Others do not really understand what is going on.

Right before the blasts, Quelana goes into Fleece's quarters. He is sitting up on the bed with his back against the wall. She climbs up there with him, sits beside him, and puts her head on his shoulder. Now Fleece thinks about Quelana often, but until now, he had thought nothing of it.

The solar blasts begin. They are in a place where the inner core of the galaxy is on the farthest side of the planet. There are two planets in front in line with the inner core. The sun is on the left side. The computer begins to analyze the blasts. After thirty moments of blasts going through the sky, not so much as one hits the planet where they are. The computer analyzes again and says it may have hit on the other side of the planet, but they will not know for another heap.

After a quarter sector goes by and the cosmic rays stop blasting through the galaxy, they realize that they have survived, and a new love is introduced. After the computer tells them that re-entry above ground is safe, they all gather together up top.

That's when Cadum looks at Teah and says, "We are going to have lots of children."

She looks back at him and with a quivering voice says, "Okay."

That's when Quelana looks at Fleece and says, "We are going to have lots of kids, too."

Fleece looks at Quelana's dad, and after seeing his

expression,... he tilts his mouth and shrugs his shoulders like whatever she says... he says to her with a quivering voice, "Okay..."

Deep in the sinking pits, Dr. Modley, Dr. Aspen, and two young ladies that gathered into the ship by mistake remember over twenty heaps ago when their ship landed on the planet. A few short moments after it landed, it began to sink on one side, causing the ship to tilt.

Dr. Yeloven, their other passenger, was already unfastened by this time, but when the ship went to tilt, he tried to blast off. But when the rockets hit the sandy-like substance, it extinguished the fire almost instantly. Not being fastened in, he was left hanging onto his seat, dangling in midair. As the ship went down, it turned completely upside down, and when it did, he had no way to hang on. He had to let go, striking him against the bulkhead and giving him a head injury. He perished.

When the young girls saw this, they began to scream with terror. As the ship did another roll, they thought to themselves, "This is it. We are gonna die."

After the third time of spinning around, Dr. Yeloven's body landed in between the two girls as they screamed horribly one last time. The ship hit on two legs, leaving it at a full tilt. After a few moments, it began to rock upright on the four legs. When the other two legs hit, it sat securely on what they believed to be the bottom of the sinking pit.

After twenty heaps went by, they finally figured out a way to get the ship out of the sinking mire or mud-like substance. It was quite ingenius. It only took twenty heaps to figure it out. Before this, they had tried everything: crawling along the bottom, rovering, everything. Nothing worked. The rovers jammed and locked up. One of the robotic arms broke.

Then, Dr. Crue Aspen realized that because the arms were long enough that he could put them in the cracks of the cliff on one arm, causing pressure by pushing to the side with the other arm in another crack while the third arm went to a higher elevation to find another crack and the arms pulled the ship up. Although they couldn't see anything, the computer could feel its way and navigate to each crack. Then, they could repeat the same process over and over again. It was a very difficult and long procedure. It took almost almost eight heaps.

After twenty-eight long heaps, they finally reach the surface. There is no one. The antennae on the radio communications is damaged, and after several leans, repairs are started by finding the materials needed to repair it with. Now, one spot, Crue takes the young ladies with him to look for materials to rebuild the radio communications.

Baraza is the name of one. She is a middle-aged woman, a mathematical analyst. She has created several mathematical languages among the hundreds scientists in recent heaps have written, but hers is the simplest. She calls it shorthand math. Everything Baraza looks at is mathematical to her. She crunches numbers for every cylinder she sees, every cube, every rectangle, every triangle, so she can't think very much outside of this realm.

As they are walking, Baraza is looking way up ahead into a small clearing that you can only see when you come over the hills if the area is clear when you come up over. She is the last one in the line. A small breeze had blown from the clearing ahead and blew limbs out of the way of about a thousand yards. Up ahead, she sees what she thinks to be a big pile of some sort of material.

After they travel another hundred yards or so, they have changed positions to where Baya is in back and can see this, too.

Baya is another scientist. She is the youngest among them. She was very young when they landed. After being in cryogenics for several heaps, when she was woke up, she took up photography. It just so happens as she comes over the hill at this particular time, she snaps a picture of what is ahead. This includes Dr. Crue and Baraza.

She says, "I got a good one, Crue. It's a beautiful background. Take a look at this." She takes her pad out of her pack. Her solar powered camera had downloaded its images to her personal pad. She brings up the picture she has just taken.

Crue, when seeing the picture, notices something in the background, but it seems to be levitating four feet off the ground. That's when he takes the pad away from her. When he does, her eyes get big, almost as if she has done something wrong.

He says, "Oh, my God!" with a horrified look upon his face.

Shocked, she says, "What did I do?"

That's when he takes his fingers and spreads them apart on the screen. A 3D image pops up off the screen. All three of them stare at it in terror as they say, "Oh, God."

It is horrible. Crue, being the only gentleman, tells the young ladies to wait there while he goes to check it out.

Baya says, "I'm not staying here! I'm coming with you!"

Crue says, "If you come, you know what you are gonna see."

"We're not staying anywhere," Baraza says with a stern voice. "We're either going back, or we're going with you."

Now Crue can't bring himself to go back. He has to go forward. "I've got to see what happened," he tells them.

So, they walk a few hundred more yards and then reach what they are looking for as the young ladies start crying. It is a big pile of bodies: arms, legs, and squished parts, all on a floating platform. There seems to be about two hundred of them.

As Crue gets closer, he starts laughing out really loud. The young ladies are hysterical until they look closer and realize what Dr. Aspen is looking at and laughing about.

"They're androids," he says.

After investigating further, he finds that some of the androids still have their personal prompts rolled up in the arms of their shirts. As soon as he opens up one, all is revealed to the three in 3D imagery as to what happened to the others.

The platform is really ingenius. It was built out of the magnetic materials found on the planet along with other resources. It will stay in the exact position it needs to as it floats above the surface so that it never goes into the dark or into the sun. When it was completely full from the colonists throwing away broken material, such as androids, antennae, parts of all kinds, it would automatically get too heavy to float on the surface any longer. So, when the rotation of the planet came back around, it would go into the sun and disintegrate all the trash off the platform. Once the platform rose off the ground again, it would automatically navigate to the place it was originally. Because this one was only half-filled, it kept it out of harm's way of the cold or the heat.

"We need to take as much as we can back," Dr. Crue tells the ladies. "So we can analyze and start building androids. We need to get off this planet."

Now, after they gather up supplies, the number cruncher, Dr. Baraza, speaks up with her analytical mathematical personality and says, "You know, the odds of you finding this were astronomical. I've calculated the size of this planet, the size of this unit, and the odds of it being here at all. We should have never come up with this in a million heaps of walking on this planet."

Crue says, "Doctor, you analyzed all that in the short time we've been here."

"Yes, I analyzed that and a few other things before we ever came up on this platform, which has all been a horrifying adventure if you ask me. It's a wonder we didn't have a heart attack. Did you have any idea these were androids, Dr. Crue?"

"Well, I had my suspicions after I saw the levitating platform they were on, but by then, you had your suspicions, too. Didn't you?"

"I suppose," she answers.

Now, Dr. Modley had been in a cryogenic state practically the whole time they were underground. They had figured out that three people could live indefinitely on the ship if one went into cryogenics every few heaps to give cultivation time to catch up. So, they took turns, unless one of them wanted more time awake or asleep. Dr. Modley had chosen to sleep most of the time. But as soon as they hit the surface, they were all de-cryogenilized. After he sees the parts they bring back, he says he can use some of them to fix the communications.

That's when Crue tells Modley the news about the androids and their personal prompts. Dr. Modley gets so excited. He begins to clap his hands and say, "They made it!" After yelling and whooping for a few moments, he freezes in his tracks. "Wait a second," he says. "That means we've been left here." He hangs his head and walks off with the new materials to begin his work on the communications.

After communications are back up and working properly, Dr. Crue begins to go though the frequencies. After the computer analyzes them, it says, "The communications are only going a couple of hundred miles."

But after uploading from the personal prompts that the androids carried with them, they have access to all the new data and are able to fix the radio to where it will even reach outside of

181

the planet. They stay on all the spot long, scanning through the frequencies. After an exhausting sector of time, they all lay down to go to sleep. It is rare for them all to do this at the same time.

Suddenly, the computer comes over the loud speaker. "Dr. Crue Aspen." Then it says it again. "Dr. Aspen? Dr. Crue Aspen, wake up please."

When Crue finally hears this after the third time, he says, "Yes, what is it?"

"There is communication on the frequency at around one million and three hertz. They appear to be on the planet, Dr. Aspen," the computer answers.

As soon as he hears this, he jumps up. The others begin to wake up as they vaguely hear the conversation. Morale is somewhat up after hearing this. Dr. Aspen quickly gets on the com. "Hello, is anybody there?"

Then it happens. A voice comes over the communications, sounding just as surprised as they are, saying, "Yes, we are here. Who is this?"

That's when Baya starts jumping up and down. "There are people here!" she exclaims.

"Are you on the planet?" Dr. Crue asks.

"Yes, are you? Where are you at? How did you make it? Why haven't we heard from you?" All these, along with many other questions.

"Slow down," Dr. Crue says. "Don't go so fast. We have questions, too. How can we get to you?"

"You can fly to these coordinates," she says, giving him the coordinates.

"We can't fly," he tells her. "Our ship is out of rocket fuel."

"Rocket fuel? That's no problem. We have your GPS coordinates. We'll come to you."

After they elaborate a little further, all four of them go outside the ship and climb high up on it waiting for people to come down through the clearing of the plants, trees, and things. That's when they see it, a small floating city that slowly comes and hovers right over the ship.

There is a hole right in the middle of the platform, and when they get to where the ship is right underneath the hole, the whole ship begins to rise up as electromagnetic force raises them up and puts them on the platform. They meet up with the others on the platform. They can't believe it.

"Ya'll built this, with so few people? It's not possible! Where are the rest of the people?" they ask.

That's when Que and Serena walk up. "I am the one you were talking to on the com," Serena says.

Crue asks, "How did ya'll build this magnificent city?"

"We didn't," she answers. "After we got up to the surface, everybody was gone, but this was already built. But we didn't know that until we spoke to the Planeterial ship that was rebuilt. A group of about two hundred and their androids built this city. After downloading crucial data from them, we were able to find it."

Crue explains how they happened to come upon a floating garbage pile of android parts. "Apparently, they went through quite a few of those androids," he says.

"Yes, we have several of these androids that we've built ourselves," Que tells them. "Fortunately, what wasn't taken from this city by the Planeterial, we were able to rebuild with the help of the androids that we created. Now, they are able to create more androids."

Now Crue is a scientist and a doctor of many things, as were many people on the original Planeterial station. His specialty... well, it is everything... from building things to creating things, mainly figuring out things. If it is broken, he can fix it.

One spot, Crue is messing with a plant. He creates an air tank using its balloon-like capabilities. One spot soon after that, he inflates the balloon-like tank and puts it on top of the sinking pit. It sinks down about halfway and stays there. So, Dr. Crue gets the idea to put something on top of it to see how far it will go down and how far it will go up.

He puts a big hole in the bottom of a vessel and puts the opening of the balloon-like tank into the bottom with a hose attached to it. After putting four of the balloons together the same way, it creates a stationary foundation. Then, he lets the air out of the balloons with the hose attached to them in the opening of the balloons, and the vessel sinks down. Once it does, he pressures up the balloons again, and the foundation rises back up out of the pit.

That's when he comes up with the idea that they can just use the floating city, hover over the sinking pit, and line the bottom of it with the balloons. During the time that it needs to get out of the extreme solar heat, if need be, they can sink it underground. Now, they have a way to have a somewhat stationary home. After articulating on the sinking city, they realize they can't bear to live underground, not even for a moment. So, they decide to only use this as a secondary precaution in extreme emergencies. It isn't very long before they have a small city built on the levitating platform encased in littonite. It is incredible and quite elaborate.

After several heaps, other people have figured out how to come up out of the sinking pit. They articulate among themselves how they have survived without food. Hydroponics, air and waste recycling, so many different ideas.

One of the young women says, "Yeah, we've been eating our own waste for heaps now."

That's when another young woman says, "Well, that's a horrible way of putting it."

Some of the others agree. "Yeah, but it is true. We had to recycle everything for the last twenty heaps," one says. "Four of us had to stay in cryogenics continually."

"Yeah, out of the last fifteen heaps, I have only been awake for five of them," says another.

They each had to learn how to cultivate fruit trees. One young woman speaks up about this, saying, "This fruit tree is so rich. We only let it get five feet tall. At first, it only put out a couple of fruit, but after a few heaps of producing, the branches were so heavy with fruit that even after you picked one, in a couple of spots, it would be replaced. With the waste constantly being recycled, the soil was quite rich."

One of the young men says, "Yeah, and quite smelly, too. We had to make methane filters to filter out all the methane."

"Yeah, we did, too," says one of another ship's crew members.

Dr. Aspen speaks up and says, "Well, we've proved one thing for sure, that we can live in these ships indefinitely, as long as the nuclear reactors and other energy cells do not act up and go out somehow."

Now each ship and their crew members have had to come up with some pretty intricate ideas on how to stay alive and how to get out of a sinking pit which makes some of them wonder if there is anybody else down there. Every so often, one would pop up, until the city was built on this particular sinking spot. They figured out a way to go and explore the whole pit to make sure it was clear. They decide they will do all the pits like this. And if need be, build above ground and underground cities, which they do as they are able.

By this time, everyone has maintained housing on the floating city. All the ships are gathered together and established in the floating city. The build of the new space station is well on the way. Eight more ships have joined them, fifty-three more people. There would have been more, except some had perished after surfacing, not knowing what to expect.

Now Mr. Tate was one of the three most well known scientists on the orginal Planeterial. He, along with two of the other scientists, is very excited about the data from the Limonium and the new Planeterial. As soon as Dr. Tate reached the surface, he began trying to establish communication with his family. He was heart broken when he found out they were nowhere around. But after going through the data for a couple of spots, that's when he sees it.

Captain Ronson Tate. He can hardly believe his eyes. Captain Ronson Tate. He can't help but to start crying. He was been hoping to find evidence of his two sons being alive, but he did not expect this. He reads further. Corton Tate, Head Scientist. He can't help but laugh through his tears. He has always known these two would do amazing things.

Mr. Tate looks back to when he last saw his boys and can't help but to feel a warm, cozy feeling as he sees his wife and his boys hugging for the last time. It sends chills up his back as he shakes as if he is in the dead of winter when he realizes that their mother isn't with them. She had been outside the ship when the planet opened up. He realizes then that he has lost her forever. That's when he breaks down and cries.

"What's wrong, Dr. Tate?" Dr. Evans asks.

"Oh nothing," Dr. Tate answers.

"Well, we don't cry over nothing, and I'm sure you don't either."

"Oh, I'm not crying. I'm happy. I was just in hopes that my wife had made it through all these catastrophic events. Apparently, she didn't."

"You never know, Dr. Tate."

"Yeah, you never know. My boys made it. One's a captain and one's head scientist over the Lamar."

"The Lamar?"

"Oh no, I mean the Limonium."

"You think we will ever see them again?"

"Oh, they're long gone by now, but if we had a ship, we could go to where they're at."

"Yes, Doctor, we should get busy and finish out our plans and our work on the new ship," Dr. Evans says.

Now, Dr. Tate and the two other scientists that were with him when their lab fell into the fault line are extremists. They have always stuck together on every little thing. They are in total agreement with each other, but even they are surprised at his determination when Dr. Tate says, "We are going to finish this station, and we are going to get to that new planet."

Soon after, they develop an android that can fly off the surface and into space carrying precious materials with it. The high powered magnetic suits take them far above the surface, and then the solar jet packs guide them through space without the use of rocket fuel. By the end of the heap, they have several hundred of these androids, and now magnetic shuttle craft have been established to go to and fro from the new space station without the use of rocket fuel.

It is going rather well until one of the bladders for the rocket fuel that they took up and connected to the space station gets hit with a meteor the size of a small laser pointer that every stylus has. It goes plumb through one side and comes out the other, spewing rocket fuel into space. After the bladder is pressure relieved, it lets out about a hundred gallons of this precious fuel. What doesn't freeze floats around at the edge of the space station, the part that is already built.

The androids haven't recognized the spill as of yet. But as the fuel floats to where they are working, one of the precious metals strikes up against another piece of metal, and because there is atmosphere in the metals themselves, it creates a spark. When it does, it lights up a line from where the androids are all the way back about three hundred yards to where the bladder that holds the rocket fuel is. It lights up the entire sky, taking out several of the androids and destroying over half of the space station.

Now, when the explosion happens, it pushes what is left of the station farther into the atmosphere. Once it hits the atmosphere, it goes white hot. Some of the androids try to push it back with their solar powered suits, and they go white hot, too, destroying several more androids. The space station is pushed around to the harmful rays of the sun. That's when the whole thing lights up the sky. Everybody on the surface sees it. It is completely destroyed.

When Dr. Tate comes out of one of the ships that he was in, out onto the platform, he looks up at the sky, seeing all kinds of fire. When he sees the massive fireball go white hot and light up the sky, he can only think to himself. "That's it. I'll never see my family again."

Made in the USA
Columbia, SC
30 August 2017